KATARINA

Ballerina

& THE VICTORY DANCE

ALSO BY TILER PECK & KYLE HARRIS

Katarina Ballerina

ALADDIN
NEW YORK   LONDON   TORONTO   SYDNEY   NEW DELHI

KATARINA

Ballerina

& THE VICTORY DANCE

By **TILER PECK**
& **KYLE HARRIS**
Illustrated by **SARA LUNA**

ALADDIN
An imprint of Simon & Schuster Children's Publishing Division
1230 Avenue of the Americas, New York, New York 10020
First Aladdin paperback edition September 2022
Text copyright © 2021 by Pecksterina & Co, Inc., and Kyle Harris
Cover illustration copyright © 2021 by Sumiti Collina
Interior illustrations copyright © 2021 by Sara Luna
Also available in an Aladdin hardcover edition.
All rights reserved, including the right of reproduction in whole or in part in any form.
ALADDIN and related logo are registered trademarks of Simon & Schuster, Inc.
For information about special discounts for bulk purchases, please contact
Simon & Schuster Special Sales at 1-866-506-1949 or business@simonandschuster.com.
The Simon & Schuster Speakers Bureau can bring authors to your live event. For more information or to book an event contact the Simon & Schuster Speakers Bureau at 1-866-248-3049 or visit our website at www.simonspeakers.com.
Book designed by Tiara Iandiorio
The illustrations for this book were rendered digitally.
The text of this book was set in Sofia Pro.
Manufactured in the United States of America 0822 OFF
10 9 8 7 6 5 4 3 2 1
Library of Congress Control Number 2021940685
ISBN 9781534452794 (hc)
ISBN 9781534452800 (pbk)
ISBN 9781534452817 (ebook)

TO ANY KID WHO'S EVER FELT DIFFERENT,
THIS ONE'S FOR YOU
—T. P. AND K. H.

Dear Katarina,

My name is Ricky, and I'm writing to you from merry ol' England—London, to be exact! The World Dance Camp gave me your address and suggested

I write to you before we arrive in DC. I suppose they want everyone to know someone already when camp starts!

I can't wait to get there and to meet you for real. . . .

If you have a chance to write back, please do! Can't wait to hear from you!

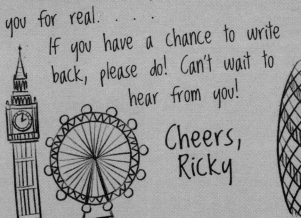

Cheers,
Ricky

Chapter 1

"**HAVE YOU GIRLS** got everything?" Katarina's dad asked as he unloaded the suitcases from the trunk of his car.

Katarina did a quick check. She had her suitcase, with two weeks' worth of clothes, including her ballet shoes and as many leotards as she had been able to jam inside. Her backpack held her journal, pictures to tack up on her dorm wall, and a couple of books. Her dance bag was slung over her shoulder. And tucked in her front pocket was the letter she'd received the week before and had already read so many times that the paper was beginning to fray at the edges.

"I think so!" she said.

Her friend Celeste nodded. "Sure do! Thanks again for driving me down here."

"My pleasure," Katarina's dad said. He pulled his daughter close and gave her a big hug, pressing a kiss to the top of her curly hair. "We're sure going to miss you." He got back into the car, where Katarina's dog, Lulu, barked her goodbye.

"I'm going to miss you both," Katarina said, and scratched Lulu behind her ears, right in her sweet spot! "You be a good girl, Lulu! I'll be back before you know it!"

"Have fun, girls!" her dad said, and then he drove away.

Katarina waved until he disappeared around a corner, and then she and Celeste made their way into the tall brick building. It would be home for the next few weeks, and Katarina couldn't wait!

After the girls registered, they made their way to the room they were assigned: 302. The room had two beds, a big window, and a small closet. Even though it wasn't fancy, Katarina knew that with the help of the posters and pictures she had brought, it would resemble the feeling of her bedroom at home.

Celeste glanced at her watch. "Ah! We've got to get moving. The shuttle is coming to get us really soon." The girls were both excited and nervous for their first official day at camp. Katarina and Celeste had won their spots at the World Dance Camp months ago, and now they were finally here!

Katarina changed into her favorite purple leotard with a yellow top patterned with stars and rainbow-striped leg warmers. She grabbed her dance bag and headed down into the lobby with Celeste, where the other dancers were waiting too. The shuttle pulled up, and all the dancers climbed aboard.

As the shuttle made its way toward their destination, Katarina stared at the huge white building with its golden pillars that appeared in front of her. This was the John F. Kennedy Center for the Performing Arts, the most famous theater in Washington, DC.

"Here we go!" Katarina said. She took a deep breath, and then she and Celeste started to follow the stream of young dancers heading into the building. They walked through a massive hallway filled with row after row of flags hanging from the ceiling, each representing a different nation. Katarina could hear different languages being spoken all around her by the dancers who had come from all over the world.

She thought about the letter in her pocket and smiled. All the dancers attending the World Dance Camp had been sent the name and address of one of their fellow attendees weeks ago and had been encouraged to write

to them. Katarina had written her letter, which she'd decorated with her very best stickers, to a girl named Mimi who lived in Paris. Then last week she'd received a letter of her own all the way from England from a boy named Ricky. He sounded even more excited about the camp than Katarina was, and she hadn't thought that was possible! She couldn't wait to meet them both. With so many new friends to make and so many new things to learn about dance, she was sure this was going to be the best time of her life!

Once they'd checked in again, the dancers met in a practice room in one of the Kennedy Center's many basement levels. Katarina felt a thrill of excitement rush through her as she walked past dressing rooms, costume shops, and rehearsal halls where musicians were practicing. This was a real theater, just like the one her favorite dancer, Tiler Peck, performed in! All the memories of meeting Tiler backstage at Lincoln Center came flooding back. Only, this time, Katarina would be the one to call this theater home for the next two weeks. She couldn't believe she was really here.

As she stepped inside the mirror-lined room, a lady with a clipboard asked for her name.

"Katarina," she said.

The woman checked her name off the list.

"Okay, Katarina. You'll be dancing in group six. They're just over there."

She pointed to a corner of the room, where two girls were stretching and chatting with each other. As Katarina headed over, she spotted Celeste in another group across the room and waved. Celeste seemed to be getting along with her group already. Katarina hoped she would too. The nervous little butterflies in her stomach gave a flap of their wings as she approached the two girls in the corner.

"Hi," she said to them. "Is this group six?"

"Sure is!" a blond girl with a Southern accent said as she reached forward to touch her toes. "My name's Myka."

"I'm Katarina."

The eyes of the small, dark-haired girl beside Myka lit up as she approached Katarina in her wheelchair.

"Katarina?" she said. "Je suis Mimi!"

Katarina didn't understand all of that, but she

9

recognized the word "Mimi." This was her pen pal from Paris!

"Bonjour!" Katarina said. It was the only French word she knew, other than ballet terms and "pamplemousse," her friend Sunny's favorite word, which meant "grapefruit."

Mimi gave her an airy kiss on each cheek. "It's so nice to meet you," she said, with a sweet French accent. "I loved your letter."

Katarina began stretching with Myka and Mimi, getting her muscles ready to dance. Soon two more girls joined them: Leilani, who came from Hawaii, and Bianca, who was from Italy. But where was Ricky? Katarina was eager to meet the boy who had written to her.

An elegant woman with her silver hair done up in a French twist around her head and dressed head to toe in black stood up at the front of the dance studio and clapped her hands. The dancers quit their chattering to listen.

"Hello, everyone. I'm Madame Maxine, the

director here, and I want to welcome you all to the World Dance Camp!" she said. Everyone broke into applause and cheers. In all the commotion, Katarina almost didn't notice the boy who slipped through the crowd of dancers and joined their group. But she met his eye, and he grinned. Was this Ricky?

"We're so excited to have you all here," the woman up front continued. "As you can see, we've broken you up into smaller groups. Not only will this make rehearsals run more smoothly, but these will be your performance groups for the final recital. You represent some of the finest young dancers from all over the world, and we believe you'll be even *better* dancers when you leave here in two weeks. That's going to mean a lot of hard work, but don't worry, we're also going to have a lot of fun! Now we're going to do a warm-up together, and then our guest choreographer will begin teaching you the first number for the recital."

All the dancers took their places at the barres that had been set out around the room. The pianist in the corner began playing a classical tune while Madame Maxine led them through a series of barre exercises to warm up their bodies.

"Psst!" Katarina whispered to the boy on the other side of the barre as they each did a grand plié. She knew she should be giving the warm-up all her attention, but she couldn't resist. "Are you Ricky?"

"That's me," he whispered back in a musical English accent that sounded almost as nice to Katarina as the tinkling notes coming from the piano.

"I'm Katarina!" she said.

A big smile lit up his face as they went into a port de bras forward and cambré back, a backward stretch. "Nice to meet you!"

Katarina went back to focusing on her barre; she'd talk to Ricky more once they had a break, but she already sensed they were going to be great friends. She concentrated on all the elements of technique she had learned since she'd started taking ballet that spring, paying particular attention to her turnout. Katarina had always been a little pigeon-toed, but she'd been learning how to turn her feet out from the hips, and all her hard work was beginning to show.

"Excellent job, everyone!" Madame Maxine said as their barre came to a close. "Now it's my great pleasure to introduce you to our guest choreographer who will be teaching you your opening number. I'm sure you've heard of her, and maybe some of you have been taking her daily classes online from home! Please give a warm round of applause for Tiler Peck!"

Katarina put her hands over her mouth to muffle her shriek of excitement. Tiler Peck! She was a principal ballerina with the New York City Ballet, and Katarina had actually met her a couple of times. Not only was she a great dancer, but she had given Katarina such good advice about being herself when she was dancing that Katarina had practically memorized her words. Katarina could hardly believe she was going to get to learn a dance from her idol!

The whole camp clapped and cheered as Tiler stood up at the front of the room.

"Thank you, Madame Maxine. I'm so excited to be here!" she said. "Are you guys ready to dance? Let's go!"

Tiler began to teach each group sixteen counts of eight of choreography that would eventually be strung together to make one complete dance. When it was time for her group to go, Katarina immediately recognized the song the pianist began to play. It was the waltz from *Cinderella*, one of her favorite ballets. More than anything else, Katarina wanted to impress Tiler and show her how much she'd learned, so she paid close attention. It was hard work, and soon

Kat's curls had become as drenched as a wet mop from all the sweat. But it was the most fun she'd had in ages!

As they learned the steps, Katarina couldn't help but watch the other members of her group in the mirror. They were all so talented! Katarina had never seen anything quite like it. Myka's elegant fingers and toes seemed to stretch for days. Mimi had beautiful expression and musicality as she glided across the floor, moving in her chair with the swell of the music. Leilani's turns were all perfectly balanced, while Ricky's nimble feet breezed through all the complicated footwork Tiler was teaching them. Each dancer had their own unique set of skills, but the one thing they all had in common was just how much they loved to dance. Katarina's group shined like the brightest constellation in the sky. She couldn't wait for the big recital at the end of camp, when they'd finally be able to show everyone the star-stuff they were made of.

Chapter 2

WHEN THEY'D COLLECTED their bagged lunches, Katarina and her group decided to go eat outside. It was a sunny day, and a cool breeze was blowing in off the Potomac River as they sat down around one of the small fountains on the Kennedy Center's patio.

They decided to start by going around and introducing themselves. Everyone had written a letter to one person in the group and received a letter from someone else in the group, but most of them didn't know each other at all. Mimi went first.

"Bonjour, everyone!" she said. "I'm Mimi, and I'm from Paris. I've been dancing since I was four, and my dream is to be an Étoile with the Paris Opera Ballet someday!"

"Oh, I love the Paris Ballet!" Bianca exclaimed. "I live in Italy, just outside of Milan, and my family takes a trip to Paris every spring. The Palais Garnier is *almost* as beautiful as our theater, La Scala."

Katarina had seen pictures of both theaters online, and she thought they were both gorgeous. Maybe someday she'd get to dance in those beautiful, famous places too!

"I mostly do modern dance," Bianca continued, "although I take ballet, too."

"I do hula!" Leilani said. "I'm from Hawaii, so that's a big part of our culture. All of my sisters do hula, but I'm the only one who also studies ballet."

"Ooh, like this?" Myka said. She stood up and wiggled her hips, making moves like the waves of the ocean with her arms.

Leilani laughed. "It's a little more complicated than that. The hand movements actually have meanings, so you can tell entire stories through hula."

"That's so cool!" Katarina said.

"Yeah, we don't have any special kind of dancing like that in Texas, either," Myka added, "unless you count line dancing!"

"Like a conga line?" Ricky asked.

"Not quite." Myka giggled. "I'll show y'all!" Myka put aside her sandwich and grabbed her phone. After a little bit of clicking around, a country song with twangy guitars started to play from the speakers. She grabbed Ricky's hand and pulled him up to stand next to her. "Now you have to pretend you're wearing boots and a cowboy hat."

"Yeehaw!" Ricky said, twirling his imaginary lasso over his head.

Everyone laughed, and Myka showed Ricky a few steps, the two of them standing side by side as they spun, kicked, and pivoted on their heels. Ricky picked up Myka's moves so fast!

"You've got some fancy footwork, Ricky!" Katarina said. "What's your secret? You're so light on your feet. It's like you're walking on air."

"No secrets here! It all comes from my Brazilian side!" Ricky said.

"Brazil?" Katarina asked.

"Yup! My grandmother is from Brazil, and she taught me to samba almost as soon as I could walk. Here, let me show you!"

Ricky took Katarina's hand, and when she stood up, he suddenly twirled her and caught her in his arms. Katarina laughed, and Myka changed the music on her phone to a song with a Latin beat.

"Watch me, okay?" Ricky said, pointing down at his feet. "It's heel-toe-heel. Heel-toe-heel."

Katarina mimicked Ricky's footwork, which created a swaying kind of movement in time with the music. This was nothing like ballet, but she was loving every minute of it!

"Good!" Ricky said. "Now get your hips into it!"

While Katarina tried to copy Ricky's fluid movement, the other girls jumped up and tried it too. Soon they were sambaing up a storm on the Kennedy Center's patio and earning some questioning looks from the other ballet dancers who were also eating out there. But the newly found friends were also having too much fun to care.

Leilani checked her watch. "Oh, it's time to go back to class. Come on, guys."

"That's really tough, but I like it," Katarina said to Ricky, wiping sweat off her brow as they gathered their things to follow the other girls inside. "No wonder your tendus are so fast and precise if you've been doing these kinds of steps since you were little. You'll have to teach me some more samba moves later."

"You bet," he said as they walked back toward the elevator. "Or I could show you how to juggle."

"My friend Michael is a juggler!" Katarina said. "We had a talent show at school last year, which was the first time I ever danced in front of anyone but my dog, Lulu. I was so nervous! Anyway, Michael was supposed to do a routine where he juggled six doughnuts, but by the time he got to the stage, he'd gobbled up his entire act, and there were only two left!"

Ricky looked impressed. "Scarfing down that many doughnuts so quickly is his real talent if ya ask me."

Katarina nodded in agreement. "Touché, but I'm still not sure how learning to juggle could help my dancing."

Ricky laughed. "Oh, I meant juggling a football. I've actually got one with me. I thought there might be time for a quick match during our supper break." He reached into his dance bag and pulled out a soccer ball.

Katarina frowned. "That's not a football!"

"Sure it is!" Ricky said. "You'd call it a 'soccer ball,' of course. Honestly, I'll never understand why you Americans call your sport 'football' when the majority of the game is played with your hands. Our way simply makes much more sense."

Katarina laughed and politely bowed her head to Ricky. "Again, touché, my good sir. So, how do you juggle it?"

"Check it out," Ricky said.

Katarina hit the call button on the elevator, and while they waited, Ricky bounced the soccer ball up and down off his left knee. Then, without missing a beat, he hopped in the air and started bouncing it off his right knee. Katarina watched, amazed, as he bounced the ball with the sides of his feet, his chest, and even his head, all without it ever falling. When the elevator dinged and the doors slid open, Ricky bounced the ball high into the air off the top of his head and then bent over and caught it at the back of the base of his neck.

"Ta-da!" he said.

"Wow!" Katarina clapped. "That was amazing!"

"Eh, it's no biggie," Ricky said with a cocky grin as they rode the elevator down to the practice rooms. "It's taken me a long time to learn how to do."

"That must have taken forever to learn," Katarina said. "My friend Ava plays soccer and has tried to get me to join her team, but I just don't see how I'd have the time. Between dance lessons and practicing on my own, not to mention school, I barely have time for anything else!"

Ricky's forehead creased into a faint frown, and Katarina worried that she'd said something wrong. But by that time they'd reached the dance studio and it was time to get back to dancing.

As the dancers settled into their places at the barre, Tiler walked up and down the rows, giving out compliments or offering advice. Katarina tried not to hold her breath as Tiler got closer and closer to her. Being able to breathe, after all, was a pretty important part of dancing! But she was so excited. Would Tiler remember her? Probably not. After all, she was a famous ballerina who must meet lots and lots of young dancers. Instead Katarina tried to focus on doing her very best as Tiler moved her way, pointing her toes just a little harder, turning out her hips just a little more.

"Ooh, nice extension!" she heard Tiler say as she came up behind her. Katarina had to suppress an excited squeal. Tiler Peck had just complimented her!

"But your shoulders are lifted too high and holding tension," Tiler said. She put a hand on Katarina's shoulder, gently pressing it down. "There you go. That's better."

"Thanks!" Katarina said.

Tiler cocked her head. "Hey, do I know you? You look familiar."

"I'm Katarina," she said. "I met you backstage at *Swan Lake*, and then—"

"We had hot chocolate together!" Tiler said. "And you did that amazing dance routine to the drums at the competition."

Katarina beamed; Tiler remembered her!

"I'm so glad you're here," Tiler said. "And

your turnout is looking much better! You must have been working really hard on it."

"I have," Katarina said.

"Well, it really shows," Tiler said. "You keep working hard and keep letting your love for dance shine through in your movements, and you're going to go far!"

"Thanks, Tiler," Katarina said.

Tiler gave her an encouraging pat on the arm as she moved up the line of dancers, offering comments while making the necessary adjustments on the dancers. Ricky turned around to meet Katarina's eye.

"Wow!" he whispered. "That was so cool!"

"Eh, it's no biggie," Katarina said with a wink, grinning back at Ricky.

This was going to be the best two weeks *ever*.

Chapter 3

A FEW DAYS LATER, Katarina was still floating on cloud nine. Katarina, Myka, Mimi, Leilani, Bianca, and Celeste were hanging out in Katarina and Celeste's room, watching some dance videos on YouTube.

The door to their room suddenly cracked open. "Hello?" a muffled voice called out.

"Come in!" Katarina yelled.

The door swung open to reveal Ricky. "I

tried knocking," he said, "but I guess you didn't hear me!"

Katarina laughed. "Sorry! I guess we got a little carried away watching these performances."

"Anyway, I just came to tell you that the bus is getting ready to leave if you guys want to take advantage of our break before the dress rehearsal tonight and go on the sightseeing tour."

"Oh, yes!" Katarina said, jumping up. "I definitely want to go. Who else is in?"

"Me!" Myka said.

"And me!" Bianca added.

"Us too," Mimi said, nodding at Leilani.

"How about you, Celeste?" Katarina asked.

Celeste shook her head. "I'm going to meet up with the Tiny Dancers soon to rehearse some more. You guys have fun, though!"

"Who are the Tiny Dancers?" Ricky asked as they all headed downstairs.

"Oh, that's what Celeste's group has been calling themselves," Katarina explained. "Sounds a little catchier than 'Group Six.'"

"We should come up with a name too!" Mimi said.

They found the bus waiting for them at the curb, and they each climbed inside while another chaperone helped Mimi use the platform to get onto the bus. There were a few adult chaperones already sitting down that she hadn't met yet, but Katarina did recognize some dancers from the other groups on board.

"Hey, kids!" the driver said. "I'm Dean. I'm a local tour guide, and I'll be showing you the sights today along with the help of a few chaperones from your dance camp." The adults all waved.

Dean clapped his hands. "So! What do you want to see first?"

"How about the Lincoln Memorial?" Katarina said. "We just finished a big lesson on President

Abraham Lincoln in my class, and I've been dying to see it."

"Lincoln Memorial it is!" the driver said, cranking the engine to life. "That's just down the road."

As Dean drove toward the monument, Katarina and her friends brainstormed names for their group.

"Hmm . . . Team Twirl?" Leilani suggested. "Or the Dancing Dinosaurs?"

They all laughed.

"Could you imagine a *T. rex* in ballet class?" Ricky said, imitating the tiny *T. rex* arms in port de bras.

"Well, none of these seem quite right yet," Katarina said.

"My team back home in London is the Lions," Ricky offered. "Lions represent courage, and I think that's something we've all shown. It's hard to come to a new place, for some of us in a whole new country, and meet new people and try new things. Honestly, I was so nervous when I first met you all, but this group is the reason I'm having the best time of my life."

"Same for me," Bianca said, as the rest of them nodded in agreement.

"Me too," Mimi added. "I like the idea of a lion being our mascot."

"How about the Leaping Lions?" Katarina asked.

"I love it!" Myka said.

"Yeah," Leilani added. "It's perfect."

"Thanks for the great idea, Ricky," Katarina said. "I didn't know you were on a dance team at home. That sounds like a lot of fun!"

That faint frown was back on Ricky's face, and Katarina wondered what she'd said wrong.

"Uh, yeah," he murmured. "It is."

"Here we are!" Dean said, sliding the bus into a parking space beside the curb. He pointed to a large stone structure just across the street. "There it is. I'll see you all back here in"—Dean looked down to his watchless wrist—"two hairs past a freckle!"

The kids giggled as they got out of the bus, with the chaperones close by, eager to see the monument in person. Katarina had known it would be big, but in person it was way more enormous than she ever could have imagined. They stared at the giant stone columns that held up the roof of the monument. With the help of one of the chaperones, they used a ramp to get to an elevator so everyone could see the memorial up close! When the group got off, they gazed up at the figure of President Lincoln sitting in his chair.

"Wow," Katarina said in a whisper. "It's incredible."

Myka was looking down at her phone. "Y'all, this says the statue is nineteen feet tall. That's like four of us standing on each other's shoulders!"

Ricky read the inscription above the statue aloud. "'In this temple, as in the hearts of the people for whom he saved the Union, the memory of Abraham Lincoln is enshrined forever,'" he said. "Not a bad way to be remembered."

"I'd like to be remembered as someone who went after their dream and worked hard to accomplish it," Katarina said. "I mean, I know that dancing isn't as important as being knowledgeable enough to lead a country."

"Of course it is!" Bianca said. "Art is important to the world too, just in a different way."

"Yeah," Myka agreed. "'I'm enough of an artist to draw freely on my imagination, which I think is more important than knowledge. Knowledge is limited. Imagination encircles the world.'" The group stared at Myka, stunned at those wise words. "Thank you, Albert Einstein!"

Katarina thought about everything dance meant to her. How she used to go out of her way on the walk to school every day just to watch a few minutes of *Swan Lake* in the window at Electro-Land. How she woke up with excitement pulsing through her veins on the days when she had ballet class, how dancing made her feel strong and graceful and completely alive, and how it had brought all her best friends like Sunny and the Leaping Lions into her life. Bianca and Myka were right. Dance was important, and it had already changed *her* life. And, most important, the connection it gave her to her mom. Maybe sharing her love for performing would change the life of some other kid who watched her, just like it had hers.

Beside her, Ricky sighed. She looked over at him and found him studying his shoes.

"You okay?" she asked.

He nodded. "Yeah, it's just . . . Do you think a person can have two dreams? Can you give your all to two different things at the same time?"

Katarina pondered the question. "That's a tough one. I think so? My dad certainly gives his everything to make sure he's taken the best care of me and my dog, Lulu, but he also loves his cooking with a passion. Why do you ask?"

Before he could answer, Leilani spoke up.

"Well, guys," she said, checking her watch. "If we want to see more monuments before our time is up, we'd better get moving. Where to next?"

After a couple more hours of seeing the sights around Washington, DC, it was time to head back to the theater for their final rehearsal before the big show.

Chapter 4

AS THE BUS dropped them off, the butterflies in Katarina's stomach—which must have fallen asleep during their excursion—woke up and began flapping their hundreds of tiny wings again. She couldn't believe she was really about to perform at the Kennedy Center! The building was all lit up, almost like it was glowing. The reflection of all the lights shimmered on the Potomac River, which ran just beside it.

"Anyone else feeling nervous?" Mimi asked, echoing Katarina's thoughts.

Everyone nodded.

"Come on, Lions," Katarina said. "Courage, remember? We can do this!"

"Absolutely," Ricky said. "We've worked hard for this, and we're ready. It's going to be a great night!"

"Let's go in together," Katarina said, taking Ricky's hand on her left and Leilani's on her right. "Just like we've done everything else."

Everyone else took the hands of the dancers beside them, and together the Leaping Lions made their way into the theater, ready to take on their dreams.

"Katarina, can you help me with my ribbons?" Leilani asked, bringing over her pointe shoes and her needle and thread. "I'm hopeless at sewing."

"Sure, no problem!" Katarina said. Broken-in

pointe shoes were a must before any big performance, and part of getting them ready was
sewing in the satin ribbons that laced up the
ankles and kept the shoes on. "I like sewing. You
wanna know a secret?" Katarina reached into
her dance bag and pulled out a roll of dental
floss. "My dad told me that my mother would
always sew her ribbons and elastic on with
floss! That way, each time you pull your ribbons
up or tie them tighter, they'll be more secured."

Leilani gasped. "Well, my dentist will certainly be proud!"

"You should have seen the cool costume Kat
made for her first dance class," Celeste said
as she stepped into the rosin box, covering her
shoes in a chalky powder. This little trick was in
order to keep her toe shoes from feeling slip-
pery onstage.

"Aww, thanks, Celeste!" Katarina said.

Her time at camp had flown by even faster
than Katarina could have imagined, and before

she knew it, she was just an hour away from the big showcase. Butterflies danced their own little samba in her belly as she and the other girls were busy getting ready in their dressing room. She couldn't believe she was just one level beneath the Opera House at the Kennedy Center, where they would soon take center stage under the bright lights. Some kind of electricity, separate from the one that powered those same spotlights, seemed to be coursing through the building. Katarina had felt it the moment she stepped inside. The halls were bustling with dancers wearing half-finished makeup and leg warmers, stage crew workers dressed all in black getting everything backstage ready to go, dressers and wigmakers carefully carrying their designs to the dressing rooms, and musicians tuning up their instruments. The whole place was alive with anticipation.

Katarina looked around at her friends and couldn't wait to be onstage with them. She realized that one person was missing, though—Ricky! She hadn't seen him since the monument tour and their final dress rehearsal the night before.

But she had to focus on other things right now. When she'd finished sewing on Leilani's ribbons, Katarina went to work breaking in her own shoes. Her preferred method involved two steps: first, using a cotton ball to apply rubbing alcohol to the areas of the shoe that covered her big toe and her pinkie toe, to soften those spots; and second, banging the shoe against the wall. Banging, in fact, was a popular technique with many ballet dancers, in order to make sure the shoes wouldn't sound loud while running or landing from a jump onstage. Soon the room was full of noise as the girls knocked their pointe shoes against the wall, the floor, and any other hard surface they could find. It was effective, but it sure was loud!

All the banging made Katarina think of her friend Beatz from home, a musician who had built his own one-man-band contraption out of

drums, cymbals, a guitar, and a harmonica. As Katarina banged her shoes against the wall, she started to drum them in a deliberate rhythm. Celeste noticed and joined her, adding a different, complementary beat. Then Bianca joined in, and Mimi, and soon the whole room was filled with the percussive music of their pointe shoes. Their own little pointe shoe jamboree!

"That's one way to get the nerves out!" Myka laughed.

After her shoes were prepped, Katarina continued to get ready. Her fingers were trembling as she tried to apply her lipstick. Twice she fumbled the bright red lipstick outside the line of her lips and had to clean her skin off with a wipe and start over.

"Are you okay?" Myka asked.

"I'm just so excited!" Katarina said. "And really nervous. Also, have you seen Ricky? I haven't seen him, and the recital's about to start!"

Myka shrugged. "I haven't, but I'm sure he's just in the boy's dressing room. And I know what you mean about being nervous. My butterflies have turned into full-on bucking broncos at a rodeo. I'm not sure what's going on in there, but these horsies need to chill!" she said, grabbing hold of her belly. "Here, want some help?"

"Oh, yes, please!" Katarina said, noticing Myka's perfectly applied lipstick and her steady hands.

Myka took the lipstick tube from Katarina's hand, turned her face toward the light that shined from the bulbs around the mirror, and expertly applied the color to Katarina's lips. "Is your dad here?" Myka asked.

Katarina nodded. "He drove down from New York City this morning. I can't wait to see him. I've never been away from him for this long before!"

Now it was time for Katarina to wrangle her big cloud of curls into a tight bun to keep it out of her face while she was dancing. Luckily, she'd gotten pretty good at this ever since she'd started taking ballet. As she was putting in the final bobby pins, there came a knock at the door.

"Oi, oi, girls," a familiar voice said. "Can I come in?"

It was Ricky! Katarina was happy to hear her friend's voice.

Leilani laughed and called, "Come in!"

Ricky opened the door, holding his dance bag

and a soccer ball tucked under his arm. He looked a little out of breath and seemed a little nervous.

"Sorry—just popped outside the theater to get some fresh air. I think my nerves are getting the better of me. Has Madame Maxine come by yet?"

Katarina shook her head. "Not yet!"

"Do you mind if I hang out in here with you for a while before I go into the boys' dressing room?" Ricky asked.

"Not at all—is everything okay?" Katarina asked, concerned.

Ricky nodded. "All good, just thinking about a lot of little things. Well, big things really. Like, did you know there's over two *thousand* seats in the Opera House?"

Bianca moaned. "Ugh! Just when I finally stopped sweating. Does anyone have any powder?"

"We have nothing to be nervous about, Lions!" Katarina said, anxiously clenching her sweating palms into fists. "All we have to do is go out there and dance with our whole hearts. Believe me, if we do that, it won't matter if we make mistakes."

"I agree with Katarina," Mimi said. "We have nothing to prove and everything to share!"

"Oi, oi, Mimi!" Myka shouted. "'Love yourself in the art, not the art in yourself!'" The gang once again all tilted their heads, impressed by Myka's philosophical quotes.

"But . . . let's try to get the steps right too."

The group of eager dancers broke out into laughter, which soothed their nerves.

"What's with the soccer ball?" Leilani asked.

"Oh." Ricky blushed. "It's, uh, kind of like my good luck charm, you know? I juggle it when-ever I get nervous, and it helps me feel calm."

So *that* was why Ricky had been carrying the ball around on their first day here! He must have been anxious about starting dance camp!

"He's really good at it too," Katarina added. "Why don't you show them, Ricky? Maybe it will make us *all* feel a little more calm."

She didn't need to ask twice. Ricky demonstrated his skills for them the same way he had for her on that first day, bouncing the ball on all different parts of his body, at different speeds and different heights, never once letting it fall to the ground. Katarina wondered how long he could go without dropping it. Probably hours, from the looks of it!

When he was done, once again finishing by catching the ball on the back of his neck, they clapped and cheered as he gave an exaggerated bow.

"Wow!" Myka said. "Between that and the way you dance, you've got more gifts than Santa Claus, Ricky!"

Ricky cocked his head. "Who? You mean Father Christmas?"

"Non!" Mimi said. "Père Noël!"

"I think you meant to say 'Babbo Natale,'" Bianca said with a grin.

"Well, whatever you want to call him, we can at least agree that dance, like laughter, is a universal language," Ricky said. *"Ho ho ho!"*

They all laughed as Katarina realized her butterflies were gone, her palms were dry, and the nerves had transformed into excitement!

The next half hour was busy with preparations for the recital. They changed into their costumes, stretched and warmed up their muscles, practiced a couple of tricky steps one last time, and double-checked their hair and makeup. Then all the dancers from the camp met together in the large rehearsal room down the hall from the dressing rooms one last time as Madame Maxine and Tiler stood before them.

"I want to thank you all for your hard work these past two weeks," Madame Maxine said. "You're extraordinary dancers, and I've seen you all grow during your time here. I know you will make us proud when you perform tonight. Tiler, do you have any words of wisdom to offer as they follow in your footsteps?"

"Remember to breathe, to smile, and to have fun!" Tiler said. "Merde, everyone!"

Soon after, the stage manager gave them their ten-minute warning. The recital was about to begin!

Katarina and her friends rushed down the two flights of stairs to the backstage area of the Opera House. Stagehands were making their last-minute preparations, a stage manager was talking into a headset as she sat in front of a monitor that showed a video display of the stage, and the wings were full of dancers stretching or adjusting their costumes. If Katarina had thought the air was full of electricity before, now the excitement was almost too much to bear. There were more than a thousand people on the other side of the heavy velvet curtain—including her dad—and she couldn't wait to get out there to dance for them!

"Isn't this just the most excited you've ever

been?" Katarina whispered to the other members of her group. "I can't imagine anything else in the world feeling like this!"

The other girls nodded and agreed, but Katarina noticed that odd little frown on Ricky's face again. She grabbed him by the arm and pulled him to the side, away from the group.

"Hey, are you okay?" she asked him.

Ricky took a deep breath. "Actually, something has been bothering me lately, and I can't seem to shake it. Back home, they look to me as a leader of my team, and part of my job is to give the pep talk to motivate everyone before the start of each game."

"What do you mean, 'game'?" Katarina asked, confused. "What kind of games do dance teams have?"

"That's the thing," Ricky said. "Lions are brave, so I need to be brave and tell you all the truth. The Lions aren't a dance team. It's my football team.

I'm a football player and a dancer. I was late and not really around today because I was working out and running drills to get back in shape for the start of football season back home."

Katarina laughed. "Why didn't you just tell us you were on a soccer—" Ricky shot her a look. "Sorry! Football team?"

Ricky shrugged. "I guess I felt a little guilty. You all love dancing so much. It's been so cool to see how passionate you are about it. I wish I was like that. Sometimes I dream of being a professional dancer with the Royal Ballet, but other times I imagine myself playing forward for Chelsea in a big stadium in front of a screaming crowd of football fans. But how can I do my best at both of the things I love?"

Katarina felt awful. "Oh, Ricky, I'm sorry if I made you feel that way! I think it's great that you're passionate about both dance and soccer. And you're more than fantastic at both!"

"Really?" Ricky asked. Katarina saw a little of

the worry leave his expression. "That makes me feel so much better."

"I think it's great that you love two things," Katarina said. "And it's not always about being the best; it's doing *your* best at what *you* love. And if I've learned anything over these past two weeks, it's that you have an extra-big heart. So you lucked out, ol' chap!" Ricky chuckled, reassured by Kat's pep talk. "And there's plenty of time to decide what we want to do. Who knows, maybe you'll be the first person to be both a professional dancer and a famous footballer!"

Ricky laughed. "Maybe!"

"Absolutely," Katarina said. "Does your football team know about your dancing?"

Ricky shook his head. "I've been scared to tell them. I'm afraid they'll make fun of me? A lot of people still think dancing is . . . well, girly. Not something that boys do, you know?"

Katarina huffed. "Well, then they don't know very much about it! Dancing is the most athletic thing you can do. I bet you're stronger than anyone else on your team because of your dancing.

"My mom told me something when I was little," Katarina continued, "that I remind myself about all the time: 'Those who mind don't matter, and those who matter don't mind.' If they're really your friends, they'll think it's cool that you're a dancer. Just like I think it's cool that you're a footballer!"

Ricky smiled. "Thanks, Katarina."

"Eh. It's no biggie." Katarina grinned back.

"You know, Myka should really add that inspirational quote of your mum's to her list." The two friends laughed as they headed back over to the Lions group, where they were getting ready to head onstage.

"There you are! Everything okay?" Myka asked.

Ricky and Katarina nodded. "Definitely! We are ready!" Katarina said.

"Group hug?" Myka asked.

Ricky laughed. "You bet!"

The Leaping Lions all smooshed together, laughing and wrapping their arms around one another.

"I'm so glad we got put into a group together," Ricky said. "Let's go out there and dance our hearts out, okay?"

"Yeah!" Katarina said. "Merde, Lions!"

"Merde!" everyone else replied.

"Places, everyone!" the stage manager said. "Places, please!"

"This is it," Katarina said, taking a deep breath.

The Lions were performing first, and took their places on the stage for the opening number. In the pit below, the orchestra was beginning to play. Katarina exchanged one last smile with her friends, struck her opening pose, and took one final deep breath in as the curtain slowly began to rise.

Chapter 5

AS THE CURTAIN rose, Katarina winced at the bright spotlight shining down on her. Though it was blinding, she was thankful that it kept her from being able to fully see the large number of people in the audience. It was much easier not to be nervous when she didn't see all those eyes staring at her! As soon as it was time for her to dance, and her feet began to move, she forgot about everything but the music and the steps. It was as if nothing else in the world mattered in that moment, and everything else just faded away.

In the Leaping Lions section of the opening number, there was a moment where every dancer got the opportunity to take center stage and shine. Katarina's turn was first. She took her spot downstage center and, in perfect time with the music, started to perform fouetté turns, which were her absolutely favorite. She turned on one leg while kicking the other out and around to give herself speed. She whipped her head around as she spun, keeping her eyes fixed on one spot out in the auditorium, so she wouldn't get dizzy. However, Tiler had given her *twenty* fouetté turns to do in a row, so the stage tilted and swam a little in front of her eyes when she was done.

Next Ricky moved to her side, using some of that lightning-fast fancy footwork of his. Tiler had made sure that the choreography would showcase each dancer's strengths in the best way. Ricky was given quick and difficult allegro work with batterie to showcase his incredible footwork. His solo ended with a sweet little duet moment with Katarina. He completed a nice double tour en l'air while Katarina soared in a beautiful double pirouette at the same time. They were in perfect unison, and when they were done, the audience broke into applause. Katarina's heart soared.

Then it was Mimi's and Bianca's turns. They were two of the most elegant dancers in the whole camp, and this was their chance to show it. Holding hands, Bianca then floated across the stage on her pointe shoes in a bourrée across the stage, looking as weightless and delicate as snowflakes drifting down from the sky. Mimi followed, gliding her wheelchair along and with a port de bras that looked as silky and beautiful as ever, showing off her musicality. Bianca demonstrated her extension by holding the most stunning and precise arabesque penché.

As the music picked up in speed and inten-
sity, it was time for spitfire Myka's moment in the
spotlight. She leapt through the air in a tour jeté
and then the highest grand jeté Katarina had
ever seen her do, practically leaping right off the
stage. Then Ricky lifted Leilani into the air in a
partnered lift, nailed four perfectly supported

pirouettes, and ended in an exciting dip.

After that, they all danced in unison, moving across the floor together in flawless synchronization. Katarina caught Ricky's eye and saw the joy in him that she felt within herself. The music rose to a crescendo toward the final notes, and they hit their last pose.

The recital continued, showcasing each group and all the amazing dancers from around the world. Before Katarina knew it, it was time for the final curtain call, with all of the dancers from camp onstage!

The audience exploded into applause, and when Katarina squinted past the lights, she could see that the audience were on their feet. A standing ovation! She exchanged smiles with the members of her group as they stepped forward to take their bows. Somewhere out in the auditorium, mingled among the applause and cheers, Katarina was sure she heard a dog bark.

After the show was over, the dancers gathered their belongings backstage in their dressing rooms, changed out of their costumes and back into their street clothes, and said their goodbyes to one another as well as to their instructors. Katarina ran out the stage door with her face still dolled up in stage makeup, while the other members of her group trailed behind her. Her dad had told her he'd be waiting for her at the stage door, and after two whole weeks away from him, she couldn't wait to see him again. She spotted him standing by the fountain as she heard the familiar sound of a dog's bark coming from his phone. Maybe she hadn't imagined that dog barking in the auditorium after all!

"Dad!" she said, throwing herself into his arms.

"Katarina!" he said, giving her a tight hug that lifted her right off her feet. "You were absolutely fantastic up there! I have someone on the phone who wants to say hi to you!" Katarina's dad turned

his phone screen toward her as Kat's eyes lit up with joy.

Lulu was jumping and barking on-screen, desperate for her own reunion. "Hi, Lulu! I miss you too, girl! Wait—I recognize that house!" Katarina exclaimed. All of a sudden, her best friend Sunny popped onto the screen.

"Hello, my sweet, sweet pamplemousse! I miss you!"

"Hi, Sunny!" Katarina beamed.

"I made your dad promise that he'd hold up the phone at the curtain call so we could cheer for you!"

"I thought I heard Lulu! But, Dad—those are against the theater rules!" Katarina chuckled.

"Hey! Let us not forget the time the usher snuck you two into Lincoln Center to watch the ballet."

"Touché, ol' chap!" Katarina said.

Her dad, with one eyebrow raised, replied, "'Ol' chap'?"

"How was camp, Kat? Tell me everything!" Sunny cried as Katarina's smile grew even bigger.

"Sunny! I miss you! I had the time of my life. We'll have a sleepover when I get back, and I'll tell you all about it! Thanks so much for watching Lu! Miss you guys! Bye! Muah!" Katarina blew them each a kiss and handed the phone back to her dad.

"Dad, these are my new friends I told you about, the Leaping Lions."

"You were all extraordinary. I've never seen better dancing," her dad said. "Hey, are you guys hungry?"

"Starving!" Ricky said.

"Well, then let me take you all out for dinner," said Katarina's dad, "to celebrate your amazing show and to thank you for being such good friends to my daughter. Myka, make sure to invite your parents too! Sound good?"

"Sounds great!" Myka said.

With their dance bags in tow, the group

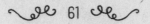

walked in the direction of Dupont Circle until they spotted a bustling pizzeria. The smell that came wafting out the doors was so irresistible, it was like a magnet, drawing them to it. It was a nice night, so they grabbed a table outside on the patio. A couple of pigeons squawked over at Katarina in her chair, hopping around, looking for pizza crumbs. She smiled proudly to herself, reminiscing on how far she'd come since her last encounter with pesky birds outside Electro-Land back home.

Bianca glanced at the pizza the couple beside them was eating. "That doesn't look like the pizza where I come from," she said, "but it smells delicious!"

"What is real Italian pizza like?" Katarina asked. "I didn't know it was different from American pizza!"

"Well, the crust is thinner," Bianca explained, "and the pizza isn't completely covered in cheese like this. We just use a few dollops of mozzarella.

But since cheese is my favorite food, maybe I will like your American pizza better!"

"Do you like Hawaiian pizza, Leilani?" Myka asked.

"Blech!" Leilani said, screwing up her nose. "No way! I love pineapple, of course, but it has no business being on a pizza. Hawaiian pizza isn't from Hawaii, anyway. I heard it actually started somewhere in Canada."

"What's the pizza like in Paris, Mimi?" Katarina asked. She loved having these conversations with the group; it was so interesting learning about the ways in which their lives were different.

"It's much more like Italian pizza than American," Mimi said. "Except for the toppings. My favorite is escargots."

Bianca's face went pale. "Oh, really?"

"What's escargots?" Katarina asked.

Bianca swallowed. "Snails."

Katarina's stomach flipped over as she

imagined a delicious cheesy pizza with snails all over it. She saw vaguely sick looks on the faces of everyone else around the table, but she didn't want to offend Mimi. So Katarina said, "Oh. That sounds, um, very interesting."

Mimi burst out laughing. "Your faces! I'm only kidding. The French eat more than just snails and frog legs. I've never even had escargots."

They all laughed and were still giggling when the waiter came to take their order.

"Three pizzas, no snails, please," Katarina said.

As they ate, chatting about how the recital had gone and recounting funny stories of dance camp for Katarina's dad and Myka's parents, Katarina was suddenly hit with a wave of sadness. This might be the last time the six of them were ever together in one place! In the morning everyone would head back home to their own lives. Myka, who was from Texas, was the one who lived the closest to Katarina, and she was still almost two thousand miles away! After two weeks of spending all their waking hours together, it was hard for Katarina to imagine not seeing them every day.

"I'm going to miss you guys!" she suddenly burst out, unable to keep the feeling contained any longer. "Promise me we'll keep in touch."

"We definitely will!" Ricky said. "We can do video calls—"

"And write letters!" Mimi added. "It was so great getting your letter before camp started, Katarina." Mimi explained to the group, "She decorated it with all these fun stickers and doodles, and there's just something special about snail mail instead of email, isn't there?"

"Again with the snails!" Leilani cried out.

"I felt the same way when I got Ricky's letter," Katarina said. "Should we all become pen pals after we go home?"

"Yes!" Leilani said. "What if we each write at

least one letter to everyone in the group once a month?"

"Oh, I love that idea!" Myka said.

Bianca had her sketch pad with her in her bag, filled with drawings of ballerinas and other notes on the past week's choreography. She tore out a couple of pages, and they all scribbled down their addresses and exchanged them. Katarina felt a little better. Sure, it wouldn't be the same as being together in person, but it would be fun to have a group of friends spread all across the world whom she received letters from. And, if she was being honest, she was excited to go home too, to sleep in her own bed, take her regular ballet class with Madame Alla, go to the park with Lulu, and hang out with Sunny and her friends from school.

After dinner they walked back to the Kennedy Center. Katarina's dad wanted to get a picture of them all together, so they stood in front of the beautiful, glowing building with their arms around one another.

"Say 'Leaping Lions!'" he said as he raised his phone to take a picture.

"Leaping Lions!" they all repeated, putting on big smiles.

Then Katarina had an idea. "No, wait!" she said. "I think it's time we change our name."

"To what?" Ricky asked.

"The Pen Pal Pack!" Katarina said.

"I love it!" Myka said. "Pen Pal Pack forever. On three."

"One . . ." Myka and Mimi chimed.

"Two . . ." Bianca and Leilani were next to join in.

"Three!" Katarina and Ricky shouted as they all cheered "Pen Pal Pack forever!" They embraced one another, laughing and smiling as Katarina's dad captured the perfect moment of his daughter's perfect team of newfound friends. Katarina Ballerina and the Pen Pal Pack.

Chapter 6

*I*N THE MORNING it was time for their final goodbyes, at least for a while. Katarina's dorm room was empty and plain again, all their belongings packed away in suitcases and the photos taken down from their walls. Mimi and Bianca had left for their flights home so early that morning that they'd had to wake Katarina and the others while it was still dark outside to hug them goodbye. Katarina looked for Ricky at breakfast, but his roommates said he might have left for his flight back to London. Katarina tried not to be sad; she would have liked to see him one last time.

After breakfast it was time for Myka and Leilani to head to the airport. When they were gone, it was just Katarina and Celeste left, waiting for Katarina's dad to pick them up for the long drive back to New York City.

"I can't believe it's over," Katarina said with a sigh, looking around their empty room.

"Me neither," Celeste replied. "This was the best two weeks of my life."

"Mine too," Katarina said. "At least, the best so far."

Celeste grinned. "Yeah. The *best* will probably be when I become a principal dancer with the New York City Ballet like Tiler Peck."

"Exactly!" Katarina said, giving her a high five.

Katarina's dad arrived soon after and helped the girls carry their suitcases downstairs. As they were loading them into the car, Katarina spotted a familiar figure walking toward the Kennedy Center.

"Ricky!" she called out, and ran toward him.

He turned around and grinned when he spotted her. "Hey, Katarina! You taking off, then?"

"Yeah, we're headed back to New York," she said. "I didn't think I was going to get to see you again. I'm glad we get to say one more goodbye after all."

Ricky gave her a hug. "It was really nice to meet you, Miss Katarina Ballerina."

"You too!" she said. "Hey, Ricky, will you promise me something?"

He laughed. "I suppose that depends on what you're about to say!"

"Will you tell your friends on the soccer—I mean, football—team about your dancing?" she said.

Ricky smiled at Kat using the term "football."

"They deserve to know how talented you are, and I really think you'll be so much happier once you've told them. I used to hide my dancing from my friends because I was worried

I wasn't any good, but the whole point of dancing is sharing it with other people!"

"I know, you're right," Ricky said. "I should tell them."

"Maybe it won't be as bad as you think," Katarina said. "Maybe they'll think it's cool. And if they don't after seeing your awesome moves, then maybe your friends are just, well, idiotas."

Ricky laughed. "I see you're practicing your Portuguese! My Brazilian ancestors would be proud. Well, I should at least give them a chance *not* to be idiots—or should I say idiotas? Right?"

Katarina nodded. "I think so."

"Thanks, Katarina. You're a really good mate. I think you're bloody brilliant, and I'm already gutted thinking about how much I'm going to miss you," Ricky said.

"You too, ol' chap." Katarina smiled and tipped her imaginary bowler hat toward Ricky.

"I think your father is ready to leave."

Katarina turned and saw her dad waving to her from the car, Celeste already buckled up in the back seat.

"Give me one last hug!" she said. She wrapped her arms around him and gave him a squeeze, and then took off for the car. "Bye, Ricky!" she shouted over her shoulder.

"Bye, Katarina!" he called back. "Write to me!"

She jumped into the car and buckled herself in.

"Ready to go?" her dad asked.

She nodded. "I'm ready."

The engine of the car roared to life, and off they drove, leaving her new friend Ricky and the Kennedy Center behind, as they headed back toward home. Before getting too far, Katarina rolled down the window and popped out her head. Her tousled hair blew in the breeze as she waved back and smiled toward Ricky as he got smaller and smaller until eventually he was out of sight.

Three Months Later

Katarina caught a glimpse of herself on the screen of the laptop as she recorded herself dancing in her room. She was pretty happy with her costume. She had put it together specially just for this video: a black leotard and leg warmers, a tutu she'd sewn herself from different shades of red tulle, and armloads of black and red bracelets. She'd even convinced her dad to let her use temporary pink color on the tips of her hair. Lulu seemed to approve too, judging by the doggy grin on her face as she watched Katarina dancing, from her favorite nap spot at the foot of Katarina's bed.

Katarina had started making videos not long after she'd gotten back from dance camp, to help teach other kids some of what she'd learned since she'd started dancing. Most days she just wore her regular dance clothes, but she liked to do something different once in a while.

She did a Broadway-themed video and taught her followers part of a routine from the musical *Hairspray*. For her fairy-tale-themed show, she demonstrated a few moves from the dance to a song from *Cinderella* that Tiler had taught them at dance camp. Plus, Katarina was having fun revisiting her memories of camp and all that she'd learned while she was there.

For this video, she'd decided to end with a simple but fun routine that she made up with Mimi and Myka on one of their breaks from class.

She struck the final pose of the dance and then looked into the camera on the laptop.

"Good job, everybody!" she said to the kids who would be watching once she uploaded the video. "Remember that practice makes perfect, so don't worry if you messed up or if your technique isn't quite right yet. Tomorrow you'll get a little bit better, so just keep at it! I hope you're all staying happy and healthy, and I'll see you back here at the same time tomorrow!"

She hit the stop button on the recording just in time, because a second later her dad was knocking on her bedroom door.

"Dinnertime!" he said.

"Coming!" she called back. She quickly took off her costume and went to her closet to get a hoodie to put on over her leotard, but she ended up pausing to look at the closet door. She'd been taping up all the letters she'd received from the other members of the Pen Pal Pack. There were the letters on pale purple paper from Mimi; the pressed tropical flowers that Leilani often enclosed in her envelopes; Bianca's notes, which were decorated with her beautiful drawings; Myka's notes, full of humor and inspirational quotes; and Ricky's hard-to-read chicken-scratch handwriting on paper torn from his school notebook. She missed being with her friends in person, but she loved getting their letters and finding out what was going on in their lives. It made every trip to the

mailbox in the lobby of their building exciting, and her closet door was almost completely covered now. Pretty soon she was going to have to find somewhere else to start taping them up!

"What's for dinner, Chef?" she asked as she walked into the kitchen, Lulu at her heels.

"Chicken à la Dad!" He handed her a plate of his specialty: a tender chicken breast coated in his secret blend of herbs and spices.

"YUM!" Katarina bobbed her head with excitement. "Chicken à la Dad in my belly! Chicken à la Dad in my belly!" Katarina sang out while she danced a silly little jig with Lulu in the kitchen. She inhaled the delicious aroma as she danced her way with her plate to her usual seat at the table.

"So how's the dance channel going?" her dad asked as he sat down across from her and they dug into their dinner.

"Great!" Katarina said. "I wouldn't say I've gone viral just yet, but I seem to get new viewers all the time. And it's such a fun way to make sure I dance every day and to share some of what I've learned. I start off with barre work, which also happens to be my desk chair, and then I teach a little combination that I learned at dance camp or from Madame Alla or that I made up myself."

"That's great, honey," her dad said. "I'm so proud of you! Sometimes the best part of doing what you love is sharing it with other people."

"Like cooking some chicken à la Dad!"

He grinned. "Exactly. It wouldn't be nearly as fun to cook if I didn't have you to eat it with."

"Well, in that case, you're welcome," she joked, taking a big bite.

"Speaking of sharing the things you love, I got you a little present." He excused himself from the table and grabbed a small package from the hallway closet wrapped in shiny red paper. "But before I give it to you, you have to ask me something."

"What?"

"Trick or treat!"

Katarina laughed. "Trick or treat! I hope it's a treat!"

"I hope you like it," he said, handing her the gift.

She tore into the paper, and inside she found a baby-blue box. She lifted the top, and there was a stack of paper and envelopes, both in a pale blue color. The paper had a pink pointe shoe in each of the upper corners, with their ribbons swirling across the top in a looping pattern. Underneath, in silver script, was printed *Katarina Ballerina*.

Katarina gasped. "Personalized stationery! Oh, Dad, I love it!"

"I thought it was time you had something nice to write all your letters to your friends on," he said.

Katarina jumped up from the table to give him a big hug. Lulu barked until they let her in on the hug too.

"This is the best gift ever," Katarina said. "I can't wait to start writing more letters!"

As she squeezed her dad around his neck, she looked over his shoulder and out the kitchen window. An even bigger smile washed over her face knowing exactly who the first recipient of her new personalized stationery would be.

Katarina Ballerina

Dear Ricky,
Happy (almost) Halloween! Or happy LATE Halloween, I should say, since this letter won't reach you until after it's over. (Actually, do you celebrate Halloween in England?) How do you like my new stationery? My dad just gave it to me, so I think I'll be writing you even more letters now. How are you doing? Things are going pretty well here. . . .

Chapter 7

RICKY JUMPED AT the sudden thudding sound against his bedroom window. He set Katarina's letter aside, went to the window, and looked down onto the street below. His friend Alberto, who lived just around the corner, was standing on the pavement, holding a football under his arm that he must have thrown at the glass. Ricky pushed open the window.

"Oi, mate," he called down to Alberto with a grin. "You trying to break my window?"

"Just heading to the park," Alberto said. "Want to come?"

"My avó is making breakfast, so I can't come now," Ricky said, "but I'll catch you up a little later, tá bom?"

"Tá!" Alberto said. "You've still got to show me some of those fancy new moves you picked up at that football camp in America over the summer!"

Ricky's chest got tight. He'd mostly managed to avoid talking with his friends about his trip to DC. Before he'd left, he'd told them he was going to a football camp, but he'd planned to tell them what he was really doing in DC—thanks to Katarina's advice—when he got back. The day after his return from DC, Ricky went to the park to meet up with Alberto, prepped and ready to confess that his football camp had actually been a dance camp all along, that he'd been taking ballet lessons in secret for years. Not to mention that he had equal passion for dancing *and* football. But when Alberto had asked him how camp was, Ricky froze up, lost his courage, and had been dodging the subject ever since.

"But if I show you my fancy new moves, how will I beat you?" Ricky asked.

"As if you could beat me either way!" Alberto scoffed.

They laughed. Ricky and Alberto were the two best players on the team, and they were always joking about which one of them was better than the other. Little did Alberto know that Ricky's ballet training was one of the things that made him such a good footballer.

"See you later, mate!" Alberto said, and then headed off in the direction of Larkhall Park, which was only a short walk away. Ricky waved and then spent an extra second looking out over his neighborhood. He wondered how different it was from what Katarina saw when she looked out her own window. When he thought of New

York City, he pictured giant skyscrapers and sidewalks full of busy businesspeople rushing to and fro, but maybe that wasn't what it was like when you actually lived there. He imagined people in New York probably thought London would be full of red phone boxes, people drinking tea, with palaces guarded by men in red uniforms and big furry black hats, but Ricky's neighborhood in South London was about as normal as you could get. Squat little brick houses on tree-lined streets, families walking to the park or the market or the grammar school on the corner, restaurants and shops on the busier roads, which always hummed with traffic. They called this part of London "Little Portugal" because so many Portuguese-speaking people, including Brazilians like Ricky's grandmother, lived here.

"Ricky!" she called from downstairs, as if on cue. "Breakfast!"

"Coming!" Ricky grabbed his football and

juggled it on his knees and head as he made his way down to the kitchen. His avó—a small woman with spiky silver hair who always wore colors almost as bright as her smile—was at the stove stirring a huge pot, and she looked up as he came in. As she watched, he bumped the ball up extra high and caught it behind his back. She clapped and whistled while he bowed. "Thank you, thank you!"

"Just don't let your mama see you playing with that ball in the house!" she said, wagging a teasing finger at him.

"You won't tattle on me, will you, Vovó?" he asked, standing beside her to look down into the pot. She was making feijoada—a rich stew of pork and black beans that was one of his favorites—and he took a deep whiff.

"Never, meu amor," she swore. "Are you going out to play?"

He nodded. "I'm meeting Alberto in the park after breakfast."

"I thought you had dance class today."

"No, that's tomorrow."

"My boy and his two loves: futebol e dança! I don't know how you keep it all straight!" she said.

Neither did Ricky sometimes. He might be a master at juggling a ball, but how long could he juggle his two loves of ballet and football without dropping something?

"Here, Ricky, take these to the table, please," his avó said, handing him two carafes. One, he knew, was filled with the strong dark coffee mixed with warm milk and lots of sugar that was traditional for a Brazilian breakfast and that his mother and avó liked. The other was tea, which his father preferred and which was practically *illegal* not to have with breakfast in England. Ricky took them out to the dining room, catching a familiar glimpse of his granddad's old football team photos and his medals and champion-ship trophies perched on the bookshelf. When he was a young man, he'd played for England in the World Cup, but he retired from the sport to start a family when he fell in love with Ricky's avó, who'd been a young immigrant newly arrived from Rio de Janeiro when they first met. His grandfather had taught Ricky how to kick a football almost as soon as Ricky could walk, and everyone said he had football in his blood because of Grandpa. Ricky's granddad had died two years ago, and Ricky still missed him, but it almost felt like Grandpa was still there every time Ricky played football and used some of the moves his grandpa had taught him. Ricky supposed that was one reason he loved the game so much and couldn't imagine ever giving it up.

"Incoming!" a high-pitched voice called.

Ricky leapt out of the way just as his little sister, Rosie, came flying into the room on her skateboard, missing him by inches.

"Whoa, slow down!" he said.

Rosie jumped off the board, flipping it up with her feet so that she could catch it. "No can do, Brother! I have a *need* for *speed*."

"Not in the house, Rosalia Maria!" their mother said, walking into the room with a serving bowl full of feijoada.

"Ooh, middle name," Ricky teased his sister. "You're in trouble!"

Their mother put down the bowl and gave Rosie's helmet an affectionate knock. "No, she's not. Just keep it outside, please. No 'shredding' in the house."

Rosie groaned and rolled her eyes. "Mum!"

"What? You should be happy to have such a hip mum," she said. "Now one of you, please set the table. Breakfast is almost ready."

"It's your turn," Ricky said.

"No way!" Rosie replied. "It's yours!"

"Fight you for it?"

Rosie took off her helmet and braced her feet against the carpet, raising her arms like a boxer. "Bring it on, Bro."

Ricky rushed at her. Ever since they were little, they had wrestled as a way to decide disputes. What Rosie didn't know, though, was that Ricky let her win about half the time. He felt like that was the fair thing to do as the big brother. But lately it hadn't been as easy to let Rosie win. She was still smaller than him, but she was fierce! She got him in a headlock, and she wrestled him to the ground.

She cackled and raised her arms over her head in triumph. "Pinned you!"

"I let you win!" Ricky cried.

"Not from where I'm standing . . ."

At that moment, their father walked in from the back garden, where he'd been grilling picanha in his favorite apron, which read MAY THE FORKS BE WITH YOU.

"I see Ricky has been vanquished in hand-to-hand combat," he said, "so I suppose he'll be setting the table this morning?"

"That's right," Rosie said, hopping up and offering Ricky a hand to help him off the floor. "You were a worthy competitor."

Ricky grinned. "Thanks."

Once he had set the table and all the food was ready, everyone sat down to eat. Food was a big deal in their family. Most of Ricky's memories involved meals in some way, whether it was him helping his mum make rabanadas on Christmas morning after opening presents, or big breakfasts like these that they had every Sunday.

"Mmm," his avó said as she chewed the last forkful of the picanha his dad had grilled. "Steven, you must have had a Brazilian ancestor, because you have mastered my picanha recipe! I'm thankful every day that my daughter married a man who is such a good cook."

Ricky's mum laughed. "Me too!"

"Well, thank you, Fernanda," his dad said. "I do my best, because I know how important Sunday breakfast is to you."

Ricky's avó nodded. "I only ever missed one Sunday breakfast with my family when I was growing up, the year I snuck out of the house to dance in the Carnival."

Ricky's eyes went wide. "You did what?"

His avó laughed, her eyes twinkling. "Have I never told you this story? Maybe I didn't want to be a bad influence on you."

"Tell us!" Rosie said, sitting up straighter in her chair.

"I always wanted to dance in the Carnival parade," Ricky's avó said. "The festival lasts for five days every spring leading up to Ash Wednesday, and it's the biggest party of the year in Rio de Janeiro. Everyone flocks to the streets, the air smells of rich food and spices, and music is played on every street corner. But the best part is the dancing."

Ricky's mum stood up, went to the record player on the nearby bookshelf, and dropped the needle onto the record inside, which filled the room with the beat of samba music.

"The dancers perform in these beautiful costumes with elaborate feathered head-dresses, and I wanted to be one of them so badly," his avó continued. "But my parents didn't approve. I was a good student, so they wanted me to study hard and go to business school, not waste my time dancing in the streets. So I practiced in secret, and when Carnival came, I told my parents I was just going to stay with my girlfriend, who was also a dancer. She let me borrow some of her costumes. We performed in the parades, and it was one of the best times of my life, even though I broke my perfect streak of Sunday breakfast with my family."

Ricky's dad stood up and offered his hand to Vovó, and she laughed in delight as he helped her from her chair and spun her in a slow circle. He tried to samba with her, but he'd always had two left feet, so he followed her lead as she swayed in rhythm to the music. Ricky's mum beckoned Ricky up to dance with her, her steps as graceful and assured as his avó's, while Rosie twirled around the table on her own.

"Then what happened, Vovó?" Ricky asked, very interested in the answer. "Did you ever tell your parents the truth about how you loved to dance?"

"I did," she said. "They were upset at first,

but when they saw how much it meant to me, they began to understand. It was such a relief to tell them the truth and have them finally see the real me."

Ricky could only imagine.

Chapter 8

*L*ATER THAT DAY, after he got home from playing football with Alberto in the park, Ricky found himself still thinking about his avó's story of sneaking off to dance in the Carnival. It must have been so hard for her, feeling like she couldn't tell the people she cared for about her passion for dancing, afraid that they would judge her. He felt the same way sometimes when he went off to dance class, always giving some excuse to his friends about why he couldn't hang out after school, instead of just telling them he was on his way to ballet.

He went downstairs and grabbed the old family photo albums off the bookshelf where they lived. He settled onto the sofa to flip through them and eventually found what he was looking for: pictures of a Carnival parade. He had seen these old photos before but had never looked at them too closely, his eyes skimming over the crowds of people in the street; the musicians and vendors; the giant, colorful floats. For the first time he noticed the young dancer in a huge headdress of red and purple feathers. She appeared in almost every picture, including one that was just of her with her arms held open wide, showing off her colorful costume decked with jewels and fringe, her smile so big and bright that Ricky couldn't help smiling back at her. Her face was younger, of course, but the features were unmistakable.

"Hi, darling, what are you looking at?" his mum said as she walked into the room, with a cup of tea and yesterday's mail in her hands.

Ricky held up the photo album. "Look at Vovó! She looks so happy, doesn't she?"

His mum sat down beside him, looking at the picture. "She sure does."

"It must have been hard keeping her dancing a secret from her parents when it made her that happy," Ricky said with a sigh. His own secret weighed heavily on him; he knew he couldn't keep lying to his friends on the football team forever about his dancing.

He flipped the page and found another picture of his avó with her arms around two other girls in feathered costumes and headdresses. In fact, *all* the dancers in the pictures from Carnival were women, just like how most of the dancers at World Dance Camp had been girls. Was this why he was scared to tell his teammates that he danced? Of course Ricky knew that ballet wasn't just for girls, and you had to be just as tough to be a dancer as a footballer, if not more so. But he did worry that his friends wouldn't understand that. Right now they thought of him as one of the best athletes they knew, a star player for the Lions, someone they came to for football tips, but would that change if they knew he was also a dancer? What if he went from someone they respected to someone they made fun of? It made him miss the days he had spent in DC with the other members of the Pen Pal Pack. He'd never had to worry about any of this with them. He wished he could see them again right now.

"Bill, bill, bill," his mum was mumbling to herself as she sorted through the envelopes. "Oh! Something for you, darling."

She handed him the envelope, and his heart jumped. Was it a letter from one of his pen pals, arriving just at the moment when he needed to talk to one of them the most? What he wouldn't do right now for one of Myka's inspirational quotes pulled out of thin air, or one of Mimi's funny stories to make him laugh. Ricky tore open the envelope, his heart sinking when he saw that the letter inside was typed. His friends always handwrote their letters.

But then he started to read, and the smile came back to his face.

"It's from Coach Dayoub," he said. "Training for the season starts next week! Our first match is scheduled for the end of the month."

"Oh, that's great!" his mum said. "You must be excited to get back out onto the pitch with your friends."

"I am," Ricky said. Even though he was worried about whether he should continue to keep his dancing a secret or come clean, he missed playing football with the team and all his friends on the Lions.

"I'm so excited for your match!" his mum continued. "It seems like ages since I last watched you play, and I love it so much."

"Do you like watching me play football more than watching me dance?" Ricky asked.

She thought about that for a moment. "No, I love them both equally, because *you* love them both equally."

"Do you think that's a problem?" he asked. "Maybe I should just concentrate on giving everything I have to one thing. Can I be a great dancer if I spend time playing football, or a great footballer if I spend time dancing?"

She gave him a fond smile and ruffled his

hair. "I think you're far too young to be worrying about things like that. Maybe someday you'll have to make a choice—I don't think Baryshnikov would have had time for a side career as a professional footballer—but for now you're just a kid who's lucky enough to have two things he loves."

Ricky took a deep breath and nodded. It was the same thing the Pen Pal Pack had told him, and his mum was the smartest person he knew, so it must be true. "You're right."

"Of course I am," she said. "Now, if only there was a way to combine football and dance. That would be perfect!"

Ricky thought. "Maybe someday I can choreograph a ballet about a football team!"

"There you go!" she said. "I'd certainly go see that."

"Thanks, mum," he said, standing. "I'm going to go up to my room to practice."

"Ballet or football?" she asked as he headed for the stairs.

"Why not both?" he called back as he ran up to his room.

When he got there, he opened his laptop and went to Katarina's YouTube channel. She usually had a new video up by about this time. He'd been watching and dancing along with her just about every day, and he knew the other pen pals were too. It was *almost* like being back in rehearsal at World Dance Camp together, knowing they were doing the same steps even though they were doing them at different times in different parts of the world.

Sure enough, Katarina's new video had just been posted a few minutes before. Ricky cleared a spot on his bedroom floor, set the laptop on the dresser he used as a makeshift ballet barre, and hit play on the video. Katarina grinned at the camera and waved, welcoming everyone and thanking them for joining her, and Ricky waved back at his friend even though he knew she couldn't see him.

"All right, guys!" Katarina said, placing her hand on the back of the chair she used as her ballet barre. "Ready to warm up?"

She turned on an old Motown song and started leading the viewers through a series of basic movements designed to get the muscles warm and ready to start to dance. Ricky quickly recognized it as one of the warm-ups they'd often done at World Dance Camp. The exercises were so familiar to him that he could practically do this warm-up in his sleep.

His glance landed on his football, lying on the floor where he'd dropped it when he came in. Why not try something different?

He grabbed the ball, and when Katarina led the viewers into pliés—bending of the knees— Ricky tossed the ball up into the air. When he reached the deepest part of the plié, he bumped the ball with his head. By the time he was standing up straight again, the ball was falling and he bumped it again with his knee.

He kept this up as he did his pliés, perfectly combining juggling the football with performing each ballet move of the warm-up.

How had he never thought about doing this before? Mixing his love of football and dance together? His mum really was a genius!

As Katarina taught her viewers a dance combination, Ricky figured out ways to incorporate his football into the moves. Sometimes it was messy or silly, but it was fun to experiment. And sometimes the things he came up with looked really cool. He had just been joking with his mum earlier, but maybe he actually *could* choreograph a ballet about a football team someday. He could practically see it now: a whole team of male ballet dancers moving across a stage, juggling balls as they danced.

"Okay, everyone, good job!" Katarina said at the end of her video. "I hope you had as much fun dancing today as I did, and please join me again for more dancing tomorrow! Remember, practice makes progress!"

Behind her, the door to Katarina's bedroom creaked opened and her dad poked his head in.

"Hey, honey, are you ready to—" He suddenly noticed the video camera. "Oh, sorry!"

Katarina just laughed. "That's okay." She turned to the camera. "I've been really into baking lately, and my dad's about to teach me how to make his famous éclairs. In a lot of ways, baking is just like dancing for me, because doing something you love always has its own special ingredients. It takes a dash of heart, a couple of ounces of patience, and a whole lot of courage."

Ricky smiled. It was almost like she was talking directly to him.

"And lots of chocolate, of course!" she said with a grin. "See you all tomorrow, and keep on dancing!"

Chapter 9

RICKY **WOKE UP** excited. It was finally the day that football training started up again. It had been so long since he'd been on the pitch with his friends from the Lions, and he couldn't wait to get back out there. When it was time, he grabbed his gym bag and started the walk to Larkhall Park.

Ricky decided to take the long way through the city, since he was up early. Wandsworth Road was bustling as always, red double-decker buses and black cabs bouncing along the street while the pavements were filled with people walking past the pubs, newsagents, and other businesses that lined the road.

He turned down a few side streets, and the top of Buckingham Palace came into view. The Queen's Guards with their funny, fuzzy hats were at their posts. Ricky decided to have a little fun. He took the soccer ball out of his bag and started to dribble, kicking it high in the air for a few beats.

The guard closest to Ricky still didn't move a muscle. But Ricky had one more big trick up his sleeve. He kicked the ball high in the air, then ducked under so that the ball landed on top of his head as he dipped low into a grand plié.

Ricky couldn't believe it, but he saw the guard actually do a very small fist pump in his direction. But just as quickly, the guard was already back at full attention.

Ricky grinned and did a small fist pump right

back, even though he knew the guard couldn't respond.

Smiling, Ricky put the ball back into his bag and continued to walk toward the park.

Ricky walked past his favorite chip shop, the smell of freshly fried chips and vinegar *almost* impossible to resist, and then he eventually passed the old Stockwell Playhouse, where he would go see plays and dance performances. Not much farther down the street was the entrance to Larkhall Park, an oasis of green in the middle of the city.

On his way into the park, he saw a bunch of the younger kids from his neighborhood kicking a ball around.

"Oi, Ricky! Come join us!" one of them called out.

Ricky laughed and cut in, dribbling and juggling the ball through the crowd. They cheered him on as he got to the goal. Right before he scored, he did a few more fun juggling moves with the ball before flashing a smile and taking a bow.

The kids clapped. "That was amazing!"

One of the kids tugged on Ricky's sleeve. "How did you get so good? It was like you were floating down the field!"

Ricky paused and remembered Katarina's mantra from her videos. He smiled and said, "Practice makes progress!" With a wave, he headed toward practice, quickly spotting the distinctive yellow and green jerseys of the Lions players on one of the practice pitches. He jogged over to the Lions, eager to be reunited with his teammates.

"Hey, Ricky!" said Adam, the goalie for the team, clapping him on the shoulder. "Haven't seen you in ages, mate. How's it going?"

"Yeah, all right, you?"

"Can't complain."

"Ricky did a football camp in the States this past summer," Alberto said.

"Oh yeah?" Adam asked. "You got some fancy new moves to show us? We'll need them if we're going to beat the Rangers in a few weeks."

Ricky tried to smile, but his stomach flipped over as he imagined how Adam and Alberto would react if they saw the moves he'd *actually* learned at camp. "Are you kidding? The Rangers don't stand a chance against us!"

Ricky opened his bag to grab his boots and jersey to get changed for training and spotted his ballet shoes at the bottom. He'd forgotten to take them out after his last dance class. He hurriedly grabbed the boots and jersey and closed the bag, zipping it tightly. He chatted with the other guys, catching up, while he changed his shoes and pulled his yellow jersey over his head.

At exactly the time they were due to start, Coach Dayoub blew on his whistle, and instantly the boys quieted and turned to look at him. They all loved Coach Dayoub. He had played for Barnet for a couple of years back in the early 2000s and had been on his way to being promoted to the Premier League when he'd injured his knee and had to retire. He was a tough coach, never letting them slack off even a little, but he was fair and encouraging, too. Ricky knew he wouldn't be half the football player he was now if it weren't for Coach Dayoub always pushing him to try his hardest.

"Nice to see you all again, lads," he said once he had their attention. "Are we ready to play some football?"

The boys cheered.

"Glad to hear it," he continued. "You all know we've got a match against the Rangers coming up. They're one of the best teams in the area, and it won't be easy, but I think we've got what it takes to beat them. We just need to focus, work together as a team, and give it our all. Now let's get to work, shall we?"

"Put it in, Lions!" Ricky said.

The whole team gathered together in a circle, putting their hands together in the center. They did this before every training session and every game.

"Whose pitch?" Ricky called.

"Our pitch!" the team cried, raising their hands into the air as one.

Coach Dayoub, just like every dance teacher Ricky had ever had, started with a warm-up to get his players' muscles loose and ready for the day's training. They did stretches, jumping jacks, lunges, and other movements that would prepare them to play. Then they moved into their drills: running sprints, passing to one another, weaving in and out of cones while dribbling, practicing shooting, working on their set pieces, and more. Ricky could see that Alberto had been working on his skills during their off-season. He was running faster, dribbling better, and making more shots than ever before. Ricky pushed himself harder to keep up with his friend. He wasn't letting Alberto claim the spot of best player on the team without a fight!

He and Alberto were placed on opposite sides when they broke into two groups to scrimmage. They even played the same posi-tion: striker. Ricky gave it his all, and Alberto did too, each of them trying to outrun and outscore the other.

"Loser buys the winner chips on the way home?" Alberto said to Ricky in between plays.

Ricky grinned. "You're on."

With just a few minutes left to play, Alberto's group was up one goal, but Ricky wasn't giving up yet. He got possession of the ball and saw his teammate Liam break away from the defender who had been guarding him. His feet moved like lightning, dancing on the grass. It was as if he were floating off the ground with the way he moved the ball back and forth with his fancy footwork, in and out of defenders. Ricky passed the ball to Liam, who gave it a mighty kick. It soared right between Adam's hands and into the goal. They were tied! One more goal, and Alberto would owe him an order of hot, delicious chips (or "french fries" as his friend Katarina would call them back in New York!).

The two sides battled, moving the ball up the field toward one goal and back down to the other, neither team letting the other's offense take an open shot. Ricky could feel sweat pouring down the back of his jersey, and his voice was beginning to get sore from encouraging and calling out plays to his teammates. As the final seconds in the match ticked down, he was within scoring distance of the goal and Alberto was right on his heels. Ricky's friend Ritesh had the ball and was dribbling it toward the goal when a defender suddenly rushed at him from the side. Ritesh panicked and kicked the ball wildly. It flew high up into the air in Ricky's direction. It was going to miss the net by several yards. If only . . .

Ricky did a deep plié on the pitch. If he was going to make this goal, he was going to have to jump higher than he ever had, needing to use all the strength his legs had in them. Using the momentum from the deep plié to propel him, he leapt up into the air just like he had on the stage of the Kennedy Center's Opera House, his eyes focused on the football that was flying toward him. Alberto jumped too, trying to block Ricky, but he couldn't get high enough. Ricky's forehead connected with the football, and he head-butted it with a flick of his neck, redirecting the ball, which soared past the outstretched gloves of the goalkeeper and straight into the net.

Without thinking, Ricky automatically landed in fifth position as if he was in ballet class instead of on the pitch. He held his arms above his head in a port de bras. He quickly dropped his hands, before any of his teammates around him noticed. They were too busy cheering, or groaning, depending on which side they'd been playing for. Ricky joined them, exchanging high fives and big smiles with his teammates.

Alberto gave him a fist bump. "Way to use your head, mate! I guess I owe you."

Ricky laughed. "I hope you're ready to pay up. After that workout, I'm pretty hungry."

"Nice work, everyone!" Coach Dayoub said as the team gathered around him. "I can tell that lots of you have been working on your skills during the off-season, and that's just the kind of commitment we need to beat a team like the Rangers. I'll see you back here on Thursday, ready to work even harder. Right, lads?"

"Right!" Ricky and the rest of the team replied.

"Dismissed," Coach Dayoub said with a sharp blow to his whistle.

Ricky went to follow the other guys as they headed toward the sideline of the pitch, but Coach Dayoub caught his sleeve and held him back.

"You played really well today, Ricky," he said. "You seem a lot stronger than last season."

Ricky beamed. "I sure am," he said, thinking of the hundreds of hours he'd spent in the dance studio over the past year.

"You keep improving at this rate, and you could have a career just like your grandfather's, or your mum's," Coach Dayoub said.

Ricky frowned. His mum was a primary-school teacher. She'd danced when she was younger just like Ricky did, but he didn't think she'd ever played football. Could Coach be talking about dancing? Did he know Ricky also did ballet?

"Um, thanks, Coach," he said, and ran to catch up with the other guys, who were crowded around their bags, changing out of their boots and jerseys.

"That was a great scrimmage, guys," Ricky said as he approached them.

"Nah, it would have been great only if my side had won," Alberto said with a teasing grin, "but it was pretty good, I guess."

"How do you jump that high, Ricky?" Adam asked. "You were practically flying."

"Oh, uh . . ." Ricky felt his ears turning bright red. "I don't know."

He took off his football boots and reached inside his bag to pull out his regular shoes. But, to his horror, the laces were tangled with the elastic straps on his ballet shoes. Like it was happening in slow motion, Ricky watched helplessly as his ballet shoes tumbled to the grass right in front of his teammates.

"What are those?" Alberto asked as Ricky snatched the shoes up. Alberto laughed. "They look like the shoes my sister wears to ballet class!"

"Ooh, Ricky, are you a prima ballerina?" Adam asked in a singsongy voice.

"I think the term is 'ballerin-o,' right, Ricky?" Liam asked. He did a spin on his tiptoes, arms held over his head in a parody of a ballet position. "Or should we call you *Vicky*?"

Everyone laughed, and other members of the team started leaping and twirling around too. It was Ricky's worst nightmare playing out right in front of his eyes. Farther down the pitch, he saw Coach Dayoub watching the entire thing, shaking his head.

"Oh, lay off," Ricky said, shoving the shoes back into his bag. "They're Rosie's, okay? She borrowed my bag when she went to dance class. You guys are a real class act—you know that?"

"Aww, don't be upset, Ricky! We're just teasing you," Alberto said. "Come on, let's go to the chip shop. I owe you."

"No thanks," Ricky said. "I'm not feeling hungry anymore."

He turned and walked off in the direction of his home by himself, the laughter of his teammates still ringing in his ears.

Chapter 10

RICKY BARELY DID more than pick at his supper that night, still replaying the events of the morning over and over in his head. When he'd kept his football a secret from the Pen Pal Pack, it had been because he was afraid they'd think he didn't care as much about ballet as they did. When he kept his dancing secret from his football team, it was because he was afraid they'd make fun of him. He had been wrong about the Pen Pal Pack, but he'd been exactly

right about his football friends, and knowing that made his stomach ache.

"You've barely had a bite of your supper, Ricky," his mum said. "You didn't ruin your appetite at the chip shop after football practice, did you?"

"No, Mum," he said, reluctantly spearing a carrot with his fork.

"Then what's wrong, querido?" she asked.

Normally the whole family ate dinner together, but it was just the two of them that night. Rosie was at a friend's house, and his dad and avó had gone out. Ricky was glad to have this chance to talk to his mum alone and get her advice.

"Something happened at training today," he said. "The other guys saw my ballet shoes, and they started making a bunch of jokes. I had to lie and tell them the shoes were Rosie's to get them to stop teasing me."

His mum frowned. "You mean they don't know you dance?"

He shook his head. "I've never told them because I didn't think they would understand. I really *want* to because they're my friends and you should be honest with your friends, but after the way they reacted today . . ."

"But there is nothing wrong with being both a footballer and a dancer!" Mum said. "The two have so much in common. Footballers and dancers are both athletes. They both perform in front of big crowds. They both wear costumes."

Ricky grinned. "Uniforms, Mum. In football we call them 'uniforms.'"

She waved her hand. "Same thing! So why should your football friends tease you for also being a dancer?"

He shrugged. "They think dance is something only girls do. They don't understand how it's a sport, too. I don't think they'll ever get why I love it."

Ricky and Mum both went quiet. Then Mum said, "You know I danced. I was really serious about it too. So much that I wanted to be a professional dancer. But I also wanted to start a family, and I didn't think I could be a great mom and a great dancer at the same time. I didn't tell you because I didn't want you to think I ever regretted the choice I made."

"You don't?" Ricky asked.

"Not for a second," she said, putting her arm around him. "And I do love teaching. But I wish that I had at least given myself a little more credit and tried to do both. I'm so proud of you and how you're trying to pursue both things you love. Plus, I'm pretty sure you got your killer dance moves from me!"

Ricky and Mum both laughed.

"It's not easy to love something when the people you care about don't understand," Mum continued. "But I think you owe it to yourself to tell your friends the truth. Maybe they'll tease you, but you can't control that. All you can control is what *you* do, and that is to live your life honestly."

"That makes sense," Ricky said. He sat there in silence for a moment, staring out the window, wishing he could magically summon the strength from his Pen Pal Pack. "I guess I'll never know how my friends will react to me telling them how much I love dancing until I try."

"Give them a chance! They might surprise

you. And take it from someone who has a lot more life experience than you—"

"A *whole* lot," Ricky interjected with a sly smile.

She gave him a teasing glare. "As I was saying before I was so rudely interrupted, it's better to look back and say 'I can't believe I did that' than to say 'I wish I had done that.'"

"You're right, Mum," he said. "I'm going to tell my friends the truth."

"Good for you!" she said. "Now, before we have dessert, how about you show me some of your moves?"

She stood and lifted the needle on the old record player, and a swinging samba beat immediately filled the room. Ricky jumped to his feet and took his mum's hand while she stepped and shimmied her hips. He twirled her in a circle and she laughed. Ricky forgot about the ache in his stomach and all his worries about his friends and simply enjoyed this moment, dancing with his mum.

Later that evening Ricky was in his bedroom working on his homework when a window popped up on his computer with a musical *ding*. Ricky tilted his head, perplexed. Someone named "KB" was video-calling him, but he didn't piece together the initials or the avatar, which was a photo of a fluffy white dog. Maybe one of Dad's infamous "butt dials" from his phone bouncing around inside his pants pockets. But why would the avatar be of a fluffy white dog? He clicked the button to answer the call.

Katarina's face appeared. "Hi, Ricky!" she said.

Ricky's heart leapt. "Katarina! It's so good to see you! I was *just* thinking about you!"

"Me too," she said. "I'm so glad I was able to finally catch you. My schedule has been so busy lately with school and dance class. Not to mention the time difference between us doesn't exactly help either. How are you, ol' chap? How's merry old England?"

He laughed. "Oh, pretty much the same as always. Want to take a look around?"

Ricky gave her a tour of his bedroom and walked her through the house, showing her all the funny little things that were different from the way they were in America. There were the water taps in the bathroom sink, which had one spigot for hot water and one for cold; the electrical outlets, which had a switch to turn the whole outlet on or off; and the two-in-one washing machine and dryer that was located in the kitchen.

"And what's that?" Katarina asked, pointing at the appliance on the kitchen counter.

"Are you kidding?" Ricky said. "That's the electric teakettle! Don't you have one?"

"Nope!" Katarina said. "I don't even drink tea, but when my dad does, he just microwaves a mug of water."

Ricky stared at her in horror, and Katarina

laughed at the shocked expression on his face.

"That kettle is probably the most sacred thing in this house," Ricky explained. "I think my dad would rather do without lightbulbs than without the kettle."

Once he'd shown her around the garden and introduced her to Rosie, Ricky took the conversation with Katarina on the laptop back upstairs to his bedroom.

"This is almost as good as a real visit!" Katarina said. "I'll have to give you an official tour of my place on our next chat. I think tomorrow I'll get Mimi to show me what a house in Paris is like. But I actually called because I wanted to show *you* something."

"Oh yeah?" Ricky said.

She nodded and stepped back from her laptop so that he could see her full body as she stood in the middle of her bedroom, just like in her dance videos.

"Now, I'm not nearly as good as you yet,"

Katarina said, "but I've been practicing! You really inspired me."

She reached out of the frame, and when she came back into the picture, she was holding a black-and-white-checked football.

"Watch this!" she said. She held the ball at waist height in front of her and then dropped it, bumped it with the side of her foot just before it hit the ground, and kicked it into the air. As it fell, she hopped to the other foot and bumped it again. She dribbled the ball a couple more times with her feet and then twice with her knees before catching it again.

"Bravo!" Ricky said, clapping. "That was great, Katarina!"

She gave an exaggerated bow and then sat down in front of the camera again. "Thanks! It's taken me *months* to learn how to do that without dropping it every time. It's a lot harder than it looks! You made it seem so easy."

Ricky laughed. "That's the trick with everything, isn't it? Like when you see a great dancer and they make the moves seem effortless. Only people who also dance know just how hard it is to make something look so simple!"

"Definitely," Katarina said. "So have you told your football buddies about *your* dancing yet?"

Ricky hung his head. He'd told Katarina back at dance camp—months ago—that he would tell his friends he did ballet, and here he was still in the same position!

"No, not yet," he admitted. "Telling the truth is harder than it seems sometimes! But I'm going to tell them soon, I promise."

"Just do what your heart tells you, and you'll be fine. Remember, Ricky," she said. "Those who mind don't matter—"

"And those who matter don't mind," he said. "I know, you're right!"

"Well, I'd better run," Katarina said. "Lulu's ready for her walk. Aren't you, girl?"

Lulu excitedly jumped into Katarina's lap, her

tail flying back and forth at the mention of a walk. Ricky laughed as Lulu covered Katarina's face with doggy kisses.

"It was nice seeing you, Katarina," he said. "Call again anytime!"

Ricky closed the video chat, more determined than ever to tell his friends the truth.

Chapter 11

RICKY WAS ON his way to football practice, trying to shake yesterday's disaster with his teammates from his mind. He was already running late thanks to misplacing his boots, and he tried to hurry, even though part of him wasn't too anxious to get there. It was time to finally tell his friends the truth about his dancing. He was determined, but that didn't mean he wasn't worried, and that might have made his footsteps move a little more slowly.

But when he got to the park, the pitch was empty. Ricky frowned. Had he gotten the day wrong, or possibly the time? No, they always had training on Thursday afternoons at four o'clock. So where was everyone?

That was when he noticed the cone sitting on the grass. It had a note taped to it.

TRAINING INSIDE TODAY! MEET ME AT STOCKWELL PLAYHOUSE.
—COACH D

Ricky was even more confused now. How in the world were they going to train for their upcoming football match against the Rangers inside a theater? Apparently, he was going to find out.

Ricky left the park, crossed the street, and headed up to the Stockwell Playhouse. The front doors were locked. Unsure of himself, he knocked, and after a moment a woman appeared.

"You a Lion?" she asked. When Ricky nodded, she added, "Follow me."

Ricky followed her into the building. It was strange to see it like this, all dark and empty, no ushers taking tickets or audience members chatting in the lobby as they sipped their pre-show drinks. The woman took him down a side corridor, through a locked door, and up a short flight of stairs.

Then suddenly he knew where he was. The floor and walls were painted black. To his left there were lines of rigging, and to his right there were thick black curtains hanging in parallel lines. He was backstage! It looked just like the backstage area of the Opera House at the Kennedy Center, just smaller. He followed the woman through the curtains, until he was standing on the stage in the middle of the auditorium, rows and rows of empty seats staring down at him. Also on the stage were two lines of ballet barres, his teammates already lined up beside them. He stared at them in confusion. What was going on here?

"Hey, Coach," the woman said. "I found your straggler."

"Oh, Ricky, good of you to join us," Coach Dayoub said. "Take a spot at the barre. Thanks, Emily."

"What's going on?" Ricky whispered as he took the empty spot next to Alberto.

Alberto shrugged. "Beats me."

"All right, lads," Coach said. "We're trying a little something different today. At our last training, I saw some of you express some interest in ballet."

Coach Dayoub's eyes ran over them, lingering on the guys who had been teasing Ricky by prancing around on the pitch, pretending to be dancers. One by one, Alberto, Adam, Ritesh, Liam, and the others looked down so they wouldn't have to meet the coach's stern gaze.

"Well, I thought that was a fantastic idea!"

Coach continued. "Ballet is an excellent tool for conditioning, because it builds your strength, balance, and muscle control. All very important tools to utilize if you want to be a great footballer."

"That's why plenty of professional footballers take dance classes and why we're going to as well," Coach continued. He turned on the speaker beside him on the stage, and classical music began to pour out of it. "Okay, follow me!"

Coach started to lead the team through some basic ballet moves. Ricky saw that Alberto broke out in a sweat almost immediately.

"This is hard!" Alberto complained, his legs quaking as Coach had them do their tenth slow, deep plié.

Ricky tried to hide his smile and pretended his legs were hurting too. "Oh man, I know!"

Up at the front of the stage, Coach chuckled. "Not so funny now, is it, lads?"

"Can't we just run laps instead?" Adam asked.

Coach shook his head. "Nope!"

Ricky took a deep breath. Maybe this was the perfect time to show his teammates his other passion. He thought about what his mum had said and took a deep breath. "Hey, Coach! I have some moves that I could teach everyone."

Coach studied Ricky, then nodded. "Then come show us!"

Ricky stepped away from the barre and took Coach's place in front of the team. All eyes were on him, but it felt different this time from how it had when his ballet shoes had come tumbling out of his bag. He didn't feel like they were scrutinizing him, looking for something to make fun of. He felt like they were eagerly waiting to learn something from their most valuable player.

"Pliés are good for strengthening the muscles in your legs," Ricky said, "but if you want to make your feet stronger, you can add a relevé to the move."

He demonstrated to the group what he

meant. When he did his plié, instead of keeping his feet flat on the ground while straightening his knees, he lifted his heels so that he was standing just on the balls and toes of his feet. This made the muscles in his legs burn even more, required more concentration, and strengthened his feet and calves all at the same time.

"Oh man, this is tough!" Alberto moaned. "Do you do this exercise a lot, Ricky?"

"Every day!" Ricky said, bending down into another plié relevé sequence.

"No wonder you're so fast on your feet!" Ritesh said.

Ricky led them through more dance moves. Starting off in a plank position to strengthen their core. Followed by attitude leg lifts to strengthen their glutes. Next were sautés. These little jumps would help with agility and footwork while extending height when leaping off the pitch to head the ball. It wasn't long before his teammates were groaning even more than they did during the most intense conditioning work-outs Coach put them through on the pitch.

"Imagine there's a football in front of your feet!" Ricky said as the team did tendus, sweeping their feet across the floor. "In and out, quick, quick, slow, beating your defender with every touch!"

"So are these exercises why you're such a good dribbler?" Adam asked.

"I'll start taking ballet if it will make me as good a footballer as you!" Ritesh said.

"Still think dancing is easy, lads?" Coach asked as the boys panted at the barre.

"No way!" Alberto said, wiping sweat from his brow, and the rest of the team nodded along.

"All right." Coach blew on his whistle. "Water break!"

Some guys lunged for the water bottles in their gym bags, while others just dropped to the stage, tired and panting. Ricky tried not to laugh.

Alberto sat down beside him at the foot of the

stage as he sipped his water, and more and more teammates joined them until the whole team was gathered around Ricky. They all wanted to know about his dance training and how he had used it to become a better footballer.

"Where did you learn all this ballet stuff, Ricky?" Adam asked.

"Was it at that football camp you went to in the States over the summer?" Ritesh added.

This was it; it was now or never. His eyes happened to catch Coach Dayoub, who was standing just a few yards away and gave him a tiny nod of the head. Maybe Coach really did know his secret already, after all. Ricky took a deep breath and plunged right in.

"I never went to football camp," he said. "I let you all believe that, and I shouldn't have."

Alberto frowned. "Where were you then?"

"I was at the World Dance Camp," Ricky confessed. "I'm a ballet dancer. I've been taking lessons since I was six."

"What, just to improve your football skills?" Adam asked, confused.

Ricky laughed. "No! It does help me play better, but I dance because I love it too. Just as much as I love football."

"Why didn't you ever tell us?" Alberto asked.

"Well . . . ," Ricky said, the memory of their laughter echoing in his ears.

"Come on, guys," Ritesh interrupted. "You

know why he didn't tell us. Think about what we did when those dance shoes fell out of his bag at our last training. He didn't tell us because he was afraid we'd act like jerks, and we did."

Adam was blushing bright red. "I'm sorry, Ricky. We shouldn't have teased you. If I'd known how hard ballet dancing was, I definitely wouldn't have! My legs feel like jelly, and you've barely broken a sweat."

The other guys chimed in, agreeing. But Ricky was watching Alberto, who hadn't reacted yet and still had a faint frown on his face. Alberto was Ricky's closest friend on the team, and even if everyone else supported his dancing, Ricky wouldn't feel like he was really accepted unless Alberto did too.

"Alberto?" he said. "Are you mad I didn't tell you the truth sooner?"

Alberto shook his head. "No, I've just got one question for you."

Ricky swallowed nervously. "What is it?"

Alberto stood, crossed to the speaker, and put the music back on. "Are you *finally* going to show us your new moves now?"

Ricky laughed, but to his surprise, everyone on the team started clapping and cheering him on. "Are you serious?" he said.

"Of course I am!" Alberto said. "Now that I know the only reason you're better at football than me is because you also dance, I need to see how good a dancer you are so that I can get to be that good too!"

Ricky looked over to Coach Dayoub, who grinned and gave him a nod. Ricky got to his feet.

"Okay," he said. "Check it out."

As Ricky moved upstage, a couple of his teammates dragged the barres out of the way, clearing an area for him to dance. Then all the guys gathered at the foot of the stage to watch. As Ricky prepared to dance, the stage lights suddenly popped on, and he caught a glimpse of Emily, the house manager, in the lighting booth, grinning at him.

With the next downbeat of the music, the spotlight and the eyes of his teammates on him, Ricky began to dance. He was doing a routine he had first learned at World Dance Camp. It was also fresh in his mind because Katarina had just taught the steps to her viewers in her latest dance video. Ricky threw himself into the steps, wanting to show his teammates what he'd been working on all these years, wanting to prove to them that dance was just as athletic and skilled as football.

He began adding to the routine, embellishing the choreography to show off a little. He only got glimpses of his friends' faces while he was dancing, but he saw them beginning to smile and some of their jaws beginning to drop wide open. As the music reached a crescendo, Ricky went into a series of à la seconde turns, spinning faster and faster, and then he hit a big finishing pose right as the last beat of the music played, his arms outstretched with his head back, basking in the glow of the spotlight.

For a moment there was total silence. Fear gripped Ricky.

But then the team exploded into whoops and applause as they rushed up to him, patted him on the back, and high-fived him.

"That was amazing, mate!" Alberto said.

"How do you spin like that without getting dizzy?" Adam asked.

Ricky beamed as the team showered him with praise and more questions.

Then the sharp blow of a whistle cut through the noise, and everyone fell silent. They turned to look at Coach Dayoub.

"Do you know what a team leader is, lads?" Coach asked. "It's not necessarily the best player. It's someone who works hard, always does their best and strives to improve, and is honest with themselves and their teammates. Someone with passion who can inspire the people around them."

He bent down, grabbed something out of his bag, and tossed it at Ricky. Ricky caught the piece of fabric and examined it. It was a blue armband with CAPTAIN embroidered on it in silver thread.

Coach grinned at him. "How about you try that on for size, Captain? I bet it fits."

Ricky pulled the armband up onto the sleeve of his jersey as the team cheered.

Chapter 12

AS RICKY WALKED to the park, there was an extra spring in his step. Not only was it the day of the big match, but he was wearing his newly earned captain badge on his arm and his teammates had accepted him for who he really was. He hadn't felt this good since his time in DC with the Pen Pal Pack.

When he reached the pitch, he found the other members of the team warming up. But they weren't stretching on the sidelines or doing sprints. They were standing in a line, doing pliés and relevés. Ricky laughed.

"I'm glad you've all taken to ballet," he said, "but maybe we should try some football warm-ups too?"

Alberto grinned. "Whatever you say, Captain!"

Ricky started to lead the team through their normal pre-match routine to get their muscles warm and ready to go. Spectators were beginning to show up, setting out picnic blankets and foldable chairs on the sidelines. Ricky spotted his family and gave them a wave. The Rangers had arrived too and were warming up at the opposite end of the field, and Ricky couldn't help but watch them. They looked tough, all right. They were kitted out in black jerseys, and they performed their warm-ups with lightning speed and precision. Their coach seemed tough too, barking out orders and blasting away on his whistle. Ricky was suddenly extra glad for Coach Dayoub.

Just before the match was due to start, Coach Dayoub had the team circle around for his customary pep talk.

"I'm really proud of you lads," he said, "no matter what happens on the pitch today. You've worked so hard and really come together as a team, and that's what matters. But if you all focus and play your very best, I also think we can win this match. So what do you say, Lions?"

"Let's do it!" Ritesh said, and the rest of the team cheered.

"Hands in!" Ricky said, and everyone gathered close to put their hands together in the center of the circle. "Whose pitch?"

"Our pitch!" they shouted, throwing their hands up in the air.

As everyone else went to take their positions for the start of the match, Ricky approached Coach Dayoub.

"Hey, Coach," he said. "I just wanted to thank

you. For backing me up when it came to the whole dancing thing."

"Of course," Coach told him. "No one should make fun of anyone for doing what they love. And not to mention, you're incredible at it!"

"Did you know?" Ricky asked. "That I was a dancer?"

Coach Dayoub smiled. "You've always had the best footwork on the team. I figured you had followed in your mum's footsteps, so to speak."

Ricky grinned. "You knew my mum danced too?"

He laughed. "London may be a big city, but Little Portugal is more like a small town! We went to school together, and I always used to see her dancing in the Carnival parade in Notting Hill."

Ricky felt super proud that his mum was known for her awesome dancing. Maybe some-day he'd make it big for the both of them.

Coach clapped his hands. "Okay, guys! It's go time!"

Ricky shook his head. There was no time to think about his future dance dreams now. It was time to go for his other dream on the pitch.

He ran out onto the pitch, taking his position at left striker, and then the match was on! Ricky and the other Lions were playing their hardest, but soon the Rangers were up by two goals. No matter what the Lions tried, the other team seemed to be one step ahead of them, running just a little faster, shooting just a little harder and more precise. Ricky could feel his frustration growing, and he could see it on the faces of his teammates.

Alberto, who was red in the face, growled when he missed a pass. Adam slammed his fist into the grass when one of the Rangers kicked the ball past him into the goal. Ricky realized that the Lions wanted to win so badly that it was actually hurting their playing. As soon as they broke for half-time, he called his teammates to a meeting on the sideline.

"Maybe we should have focused more on football training instead of ballet," Adam snapped once they were in a huddle. "We're getting killed out there!"

"The ballet isn't the problem," Ricky said. "We're just getting flustered. We need to calm down and play like we know we're able to. Like this is a scrimmage between us and not a game against another team. Got it?"

Everyone nodded.

"Lead the way, Captain," Alberto added.

They went back out onto the pitch, and Ricky took a deep breath. He just needed to play the same way he danced, with confidence, fluidity, and grace. The ref blew the whistle to resume the game, and Ricky was off, dashing down the pitch. Alberto had the ball, expertly dribbling it between two defenders. His footwork was almost as fast as Ricky's, so maybe the ballet training was helping after all! Ritesh ran for the goal, and Alberto sent the ball sailing toward him. Ritesh did a deep plié and then leapt high into the air, above the defender trying to block him. He head-butted the ball, sending it right into the goal, and the spectators on the side-lines broke into cheers.

The Lions were getting their confidence back. They battled the Rangers toe-to-toe, the lead changing hands several times as each team racked up goals. As the final minutes of the game ticked down, the teams were tied. Just one more goal and the Lions could actually win this thing! Alberto passed Ricky the ball, but there was a big defender between him and the net. Ricky spun on his toes, trying to fool the other player and get past him, but the other boy stuck a foot out and tripped him. Ricky went sprawling to the grass.

"This is football, mate, not dance class!" the boy said as the ref blew his whistle.

Ricky suddenly had an idea. As the ref pulled a yellow card from his back pocket to warn the Ranger player for tripping Ricky, Alberto ran over to help Ricky up.

"You hurt?" Alberto asked.

"No, but listen to this," Ricky said.

While the Rangers player argued with the ref, Ricky and Alberto quickly grabbed a couple of their teammates, and Ricky explained his plan.

"Are you *serious*?" Alberto said when Ricky had told them his idea.

"We'll be laughed off the pitch!" Liam added.

"I think it's brilliant," Ritesh said. "And it might just work."

"We've got less than a minute of playing time left to score," Ricky said. "At least this gives us a chance. But it's up to you guys. What do you say?"

"I say let's try it!" Ritesh said.

Alberto nodded. "Yeah, it's worth a shot."

The Rangers player had finally settled down, and the ref blew his whistle to resume play.

Ricky and the other boys hurried back to their positions. He could see the nervousness in their eyes, and he felt it too. The butterflies from dance camp in DC were back, but he thought this stunt might just work. If not, though, the team might lose all their faith in him as their new captain. And they very well might be laughed off the pitch. Not only from the opposing team but also from the spectators.

But it was a risk Ricky was willing to take.

The Lions had possession of the ball as they lined up for the set piece, tightly guarded by the Rangers' defense. This was it, now or never!

"Five, six, seven, eight!" Ricky cried.

In unison, he and the other members of the team broke out into the short dance combination from Katarina's video that Ricky had taught them at the theater. While they stepped and spun, the Rangers' defense, who had been guarding them, stopped dead in their tracks and stared at the Lions in confusion. In fact, *all* of the Rangers players stopped with their jaws dropped to watch them dance.

Ricky seized the opportunity and ran past the shocked Rangers' defense, toward the opposite goal. As Alberto saw Ricky streaking toward the goal, Ricky shouted, "Now!"

Ritesh surged forward and booted the ball, sending it soaring over the Rangers' defense. The Rangers defenders ran after Ricky, but that moment of frozen shock had put them behind. They were closing in on Ricky with the ball now at his feet, but they wouldn't have had time to catch him before he was able to pass the ball over to Alberto, who was now wide open on the opposite side of the pitch.

As Alberto received the pass, Ricky was stopped short by the Rangers' biggest defender, who had caught up to him and was now sticking on him like glue. There was no getting around him. The guy was like a brick wall. As Alberto dribbled down the side of the pitch, Ricky struggled to get open, but it was no use. As Ricky struggled, so did Alberto with the defenders now closing in on him. Suddenly Ricky had an idea that struck him like lightning.

He began executing coupé jetés to slip and spin around the defender, while at the same time giving him enough room to potentially shoot the ball in stride, if only Alberto could cross it his way.

Ricky was still far away from the Rangers' goal, so he was going to need all the momentum he could muster behind him when he took his shot. With Alberto's precision and skilled footwork, he managed to slip the ball right between the legs of the two defenders as he maneuvered what looked like a a chaîné turn to spin past them. He was free! Nothing but open pitch, Ricky, and the keeper lay before him! Alberto spotted his captain—Ricky—wide open in the middle of the box, spinning like a top as the defense looked on, this time not in shock but impressed. One of the Rangers defenders, without realizing, even started to applaud.

Alberto gave a determined grin and launched the ball toward Ricky, high into the air, and with his final turn, Ricky kicked it in stride with the back of his heel. Giving it all his might.

Everyone watching seemed to hold their breath as the ball flew toward the net. The goalie leapt, arms outstretched, but the ball

flew just beyond his reach, right into the corner of the net.

The crowd roared! Ricky collapsed to his knees on the pitch as the whistle blew, marking the end of the match, and moments later his teammates were surrounding him, helping him up and giving him high fives. They'd done it! They'd actually won!

"That was amazing, Ricky!" Alberto said.

Adam was laughing. "Did you see their faces? They couldn't figure out what was going on when you all started dancing!"

"Well done, lads!" Coach Dayoub said. "That's not quite how I *thought* you were going to use your dance training, but it worked! Let's give Ricky a hand for his leadership today. That move took a lot of guts, and the team couldn't have done it without you."

"Three cheers for our captain!" Alberto said. "Hip, hip!"

"Hooray!" the team shouted as Adam and

Ritesh hoisted Ricky onto their shoulders!

Ricky felt like he was floating on air as he finished celebrating with his team and joined his family on the sidelines. They all gave him big hugs and congratulated him on his match-winning goal.

"That was a pretty neat trick!" Rosie said. "Think we'll ever see the pros try that?"

Ricky grinned. "Maybe someday, when I'm playing for them."

"Querido!" his avó said. "I'm so proud of you! You played so well, and your turns were beautiful!"

"Let's go home!" Mum said. "It's almost time for supper."

"Yeah, after that match I'm starving!" Ricky said. "What are we having?"

"Moqueca," Avó said. It was her specialty, a delicious Brazilian fish stew. "And we'll stop at the shop for some good old-fashioned chips to go with it—how does that sound?"

"Perfect!" Ricky said, gathering his things to go.

"Oh, I almost forgot." Ricky's dad reached into his back pocket and pulled out an envelope, which he handed to Ricky. "This came in the mail for you."

Ricky glanced down at the envelope, recognizing Katarina's handwriting even before he saw her name in the top left corner.

"Thanks!" he said. He put the envelope in his backpack so that he could read the letter later. Ricky smiled as he gently placed the letter next to his football boots and his ballet shoes. All the things he loved in one place.

Acknowledgments

STORYBOOKS HAVE THE INCREDIBLE power to move children and shape the way they feel and interact with the world. Tiler remembers reading her favorite book about dance over and over again as a little girl and being enchanted by the idea that dance is a universal language that has the ability to move everyone too. When Kyle was little, he took a dance class and locked himself inside a bathroom the day he found out he had to perform in a recital. To this day, he wonders what might have been if he had seen it through. We are hoping that this book will inspire kids of all ages to own what makes them unique and embrace their own special gifts. Work hard, be kind, and dream big, and you'll be amazed at what's possible!

We want to extend a special thank-you to Alyson Heller and the entire Aladdin/Simon & Schuster team—Mara Anastas, Chriscynethia Floyd, Valerie Garfield, Kristin Gilson, Tiara Iandiorio, Chelsea Morgan, Nicole Russo, Lauren Carr, Caitlin Sweeny, Alissa Nigro, and Anna Jarzab—for making our dreams a reality. You surrounded us with so much warmth and guidance, and we knew from our first meeting: *Katarina Ballerina* had found the dream team. We're so incredibly grateful for you all and for the opportunity to bring her to life once again.

To our agent, Lacy Lynch, and to Dabney Rice of Dupree Miller, for your tireless work and support. You believed in us as authors and in our book from the very beginning, and we couldn't have done this without your guidance and passion for storytelling.

To Cristin Terrill, Sumiti Collina, and Sara Luna, thank you for hearing our voices and pouring your heart into the story and illustrations to help us bring Katarina to life.

Kyle would like to personally thank his mom and dad along with all the other parents in his life. From his close friends to his extended family, who each have their own little ones to read and share stories with—this book is motivated by your example and heart. You are all stellar role models, and I can only hope that our story will inspire you and your little ones as much as you all have inspired me.

Tiler would also like to thank Lauren Auslander and her LUNA team for being the link that made all of this possible. Thank you for always pushing me to dream big and then making those dreams become realities.

Victoria Morris, for always having my best interests at heart. You have been by my side since I was eight years old, and I look forward to many more years of friendship.

Finally, to the one constant in my life: my family. Your unwavering love and support is something I feel grateful for every day. Thank you, Grandma, for your dedication to my training and encouragement to live a life beyond what you had. My mother, who introduced me to my love of dance and continued to guide and support me every step of the way. My dad, for always being the rock for us girls. And to my sister, Myka, who has been the best role model a sister could ask for. Your strength and selflessness astound me every day.

My father actually met my mother while he was coaching football at Utah State and while she was dancing there during the summer. Shortly thereafter, he started making his players take dance to improve their footwork and saw a big difference. Thank you for teaching and showing me the power of dance and its ability to move people from such a young age. Your encouragement to view dancers as some of the best athletes along with my love of watching Myka play soccer all the way throughout college helped inspire this book! I love you all!

DON'T MISS KATARINA'S FIRST ADVENTURE!

"**D**AD!" **KATARINA CRIED.** She'd been battling her hair for so long that her arms were starting to go numb from holding them over her head. No matter what she did, she couldn't get her curls under control. "I need your help!"

"Never fear, Dad is here!" he said in the deep, silly superhero voice of his that always made Katarina laugh. He squeezed into the tiny bathroom behind her and kissed the top of her head. "What's up, buttercup?"

"Can you put my hair in a ponytail?" She handed him the comb and hair tie. "A nice smooth one with no bumps on top?" That was how the other girls at school did *their* hair. Stef and Darci had started it, and now everyone wore their hair in the tightest, slickest ponytail they could manage. Too bad Katarina's cloud of curls didn't want to cooperate.

"I can try, sweetie," her dad said, getting to work. He'd gotten a lot better at doing her hair over the past couple of years. "But why not just wear it down today? You have such beautiful hair."

Katarina sighed. He would never understand. He was always telling her she was extraordinary, which was really sweet and exactly the kind of thing a good dad *should* say. But all Katarina wanted, just for once, was to fit in.

"I think that's the best I can do," he said after he'd wrestled her hair into a ponytail. It was still bumpy on top—not like the smooth, glossy

ponytails Stef and Darci wore—but it was probably as good as it was going to get. "Come on,
breakfast is almost ready."

Katarina gave herself one last look in the mirror before the heavenly smell of cooking bacon
made her forget her hair and sprint for the
table. Her dad went back to the stove, poking
at the bacon with a spatula. Their dog, Lulu, a
fluffy Maltipoo with big brown eyes, was sitting

at his feet, trembling with concentration as she watched his every move, hoping he'd drop one of the bacon strips.

"Oops!" he said, deliberately dropping a piece onto the floor like he always did. Lulu pounced on it, gobbling it up with glee. Katarina laughed. She liked bacon too, but Lulu loved it more than anything else in the world.

"How can you even taste it when you eat that fast, Lulu?" she asked. The dog just cocked her head and blinked up at her.

"Here you go, sweetie," her dad said as he handed her a plate containing the Dad Special: a smiley face made of two eggs over easy for eyes, a strawberry nose, and a ribbon of bacon for a smile.

"Yum!" Katarina said, diving in.

"How can you even taste it when you eat that fast?" her dad teased.

Katarina grinned and rolled her eyes. "Ha ha, very funny."

Katarina had eaten only one wobbly egg when she glanced at the clock on the stove and dropped her fork.

"Oh man!" she said. "I've got to go!" She hadn't realized how much time she'd spent doing battle with her hair.

"What's the hurry?" her dad asked. "You've still got plenty of time before school starts. You haven't even touched your mouth!" He gestured at the strip of bacon on her plate.

"I want to get there early," she said, swinging her bag onto her back and wrapping her scarf around her neck. She grabbed the piece of bacon to take with her and eat on the walk to school. "Love you! Come on, Lulu!"

"Have a good day!" her dad called after them as Katarina and Lulu dashed from the apartment.

As usual, her neighborhood of Sunnyside was humming with activity. Pigeons pecked at the sidewalk, buses rumbled along the streets, and the smell of fresh doughnuts being made at the shop on the corner wafted through the air. Katarina waved at her neighbor Mrs. Morris, who was watering the pots of daisies on her stoop, and Lulu barked at the orange tabby cat who was always sitting in the window of the apartment across the street. It was an ordinary day, except that when she got to the end of the block, where she was supposed to turn left to head to school, Katarina turned right.

This was why Katarina had been leaving for school early. Last Saturday, when she and her dad had been walking home after picking up Indian food from their favorite restaurant, Katarina had spotted it. The electronics store on Forty-Third Street had two big-screen TVs in its windows that would play the same thing on a loop for weeks. It had been a nature documentary about whales last month, but Katarina had nearly dropped their dinner when she'd seen what the video had changed to. Ever since that night, she'd been walking two blocks out of her way every morning on her way to school in order to spend a few minutes watching.

Katarina stopped in front of the window of Electro-Land, staring at the image on one of the giant screens. Four beautiful ballerinas floated across a stage, their hands linked together as they jumped and moved in perfect unison. Their tutus looked like shimmering cotton candy, and on top of their hair—which was pulled back into the sleekest, shiniest buns Katarina had ever seen—they wore sparkling feather headdresses. They were so strong and graceful, and more than anything Katarina wanted to be like them one day.

As she watched, she mimicked their moves. She stood as tall on her toes as she could and tried to flutter her feet when she jumped the way the ballerinas did. She wasn't as good as

they were, but she'd been practicing in secret in her room at night and she was getting better. She'd asked her dad if she could take ballet lessons about a thousand times, but he'd always said no, that lessons were expensive and they couldn't afford them. Katarina could tell it made him sad to have to tell her no, so she stopped asking and starting practicing on her own. Sometimes she danced along with lessons on YouTube, and other times she just put on a song and moved in whatever way the music made her feel. It might not be real lessons, but she was sure all the practice was paying off anyway. She'd almost broken a lamp the first time she'd tried to spin all the way around on one foot, but now she could do it without falling over. Sometimes when she closed her eyes, she could imagine herself dancing in front of a huge crowd of people. She'd leap and twirl across the stage, and everyone would jump to their feet to clap for her when she was finished!

"Coo-coo!"

Katarina jumped, her eyes flying open. She hadn't even realized she'd closed them, but while she'd been imagining dancing for an adoring audience, a group of pigeons had gathered on the sidewalk next to her. No doubt they were eyeing the half-eaten strip of bacon she was holding.

"Go! Shoo!" she said.

But they didn't move. The biggest and bravest one even hopped a little closer to her on his thin pink feet. Katarina looked down at the pigeon's spindly toes, which curved inward toward his body, and then down at her own. She had pigeon toes too. Whereas most people's feet pointed straight ahead, hers had always turned in a little bit, like her big toes were two magnets, always being pulled together by some invisible force. None of the perfect ballerinas in the video had toes like that.

*T*ILER PECK is an award-winning international ballerina and has been a principal dancer with New York City Ballet since 2009. As an actress, she has been seen on Broadway in *On the Town* (as Ivy) and *The Music Man* (as Gracie). She originated the role of Marie in the Kennedy Center's production of *Marie, Dancing Still*, which is Broadway-bound with Tiler attached to star alongside her coauthor, Kyle Harris. She is a recipient of the 2013 Princess Grace Statue Award and a 2016 *Dance Magazine* Award and was named one of the *Forbes* 30 Under 30 in Hollywood & Entertainment. Tiler was the first woman to curate three *BalletNOW* performances at the Music Center in Los Angeles, and she starred in the Hulu documentary

Ballet Now. She is the designer of Tiler Peck Designs for Body Wrappers, a line of dancewear for all ages, and leads a free dance class, #TurnItOutWithTiler, on her Instagram. *Katarina Ballerina*, Tiler and Kyle's first children's book, was released in 2020. She lives in New York City with her dog, Cali.

KYLE HARRIS is a Broadway and television actor as well as a coauthor of the Katarina Ballerina series. He recently starred in the Freeform television series *Stitchers* and has appeared on Broadway in *The Inheritance* and *Sondheim on Sondheim*. He toured the country as Tony in the Broadway national tour of *West Side Story* and starred opposite his coauthor, Tiler Peck, in the Broadway-bound musical *Marie, Dancing Still*. Kyle has also appeared on television in *Grey's Anatomy*, *God Friended Me*, *High Maintenance*, *The Carrie Diaries*, *Liza on Demand*, *Beauty and the Beast*, and *The Blacklist: Redemption*. Kyle currently lives in Los Angeles with his wife, Stefanie.

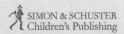